COUNTERFEIT

ALSO BY KIRSTIN CHEN

Bury What We Cannot Take

Soy Sauce for Beginners

COUNTERFEIT

A NOVEL

KIRSTIN CHEN

wm

WILLIAM MORROW
An Imprint of HarperCollins*Publishers*

HarperCollins books may be purchased for educational, business, or sales promotional use. For information, please email the Special Markets Department at SPsales@harpercollins.com.

FIRST EDITION

Designed by Nancy Singer

Library of Congress Cataloging-in-Publication Data has been applied for.

ISBN 978-0-06-311954-3 (hardcover)
ISBN 978-0-06-326699-5 (international edition)

22 23 24 25 26   LSC   10 9 8 7 6 5 4 3 2 1

For my grandmother

COUNTERFEIT

PART I

1

The first thing I noticed was the eyes. They were anime-character huge, with thick double-eyelid folds, expertly contoured in coppery tones, framed by premium lash extensions, soft and full as a fur pelt. Then there was the hair—sleek yet voluminous, nipple-length barrel curls—and the skin, poreless and very white. And the clothes—sumptuous silk blouse, patent Louboutins. And, finally, the bag—an enormous Birkin 40 in classic orange. Back then, I wouldn't have known all these details, although, like most people, I knew those bags were absurdly expensive and impossible to obtain. All of this is just to say, the woman standing in the doorway of my neighborhood coffee shop looked rich. Asian-tourist rich. Mainland-Chinese rich. Rich-rich.

Of course I was surprised. Almost twenty years had passed since I'd last seen her, and she looked nothing like my freshman-year roommate. In fact, she didn't even sound like her. Back at Stanford she'd had a thick singsong accent. Each word she spoke curled in around the edges like a lettuce leaf. She struggled with the "th" sound, so *mother* came out *mo-zer*; *other*, *o-zer*. Now, though, it would have taken me a few lines to figure out that she was from China. On the phone, when she'd identified herself, she'd pronounced her last name like the tooth. Ava? Is that you? It's Winnie *Faaang.*

Why on earth did she want to catch up? How did she even get my number? In hindsight, she must have had her private investigator track me down, but when I asked her then, she answered breezily, Oh, I looked you up in the alumni listserv.

I didn't think to question her further. I agreed to meet for coffee, a part of me curious to see what had become of her. She'd dropped out of school so suddenly, midway through our first year. None of my college friends were in touch with her, and she didn't use social media, at least not under her real name. Still, rumors drifted in from time to time: we heard she'd gone back to her hometown of Xiamen and graduated college there, that she moved to Virginia to care for an ailing aunt, that she married an American and quickly divorced. A friend of a friend had run into Winnie while touring one of those pricey Chinese immersion private schools in L.A., where she'd apparently taught for a spell.

The woman in the doorway caught sight of me. Ava, she cried. She hurried over holding out one arm for a hug, her other weighted down by the duffel-size Birkin. The coffee shop patrons looked up with idle curiosity, probably pegged her for another one of those influencers, and returned to their screens.

I'd dressed carefully, changing out of my usual leggings for pants that zipped, stippling concealer under my eyes. Now, however, I felt as plain as a brown paper bag.

Winnie ordered a double espresso at the counter and toted the doll-size cup and saucer back to the table.

I asked what had brought her to San Francisco, and she said she was here on business—handbag manufacturing, boring stuff. She waved a hand laden with emerald and sapphire eternity bands. To think I'd left my engagement ring at home for fear of appearing too flashy.

Now I know you're wondering why I called, she said. She explained that a dear friend in China needed a liver transplant and wanted the procedure done in the US. She'd done some research; she knew my husband was a successful transplant surgeon. Might I put her in touch with him? She understood that he was highly regarded in the field.

Again, I hadn't heard from her in twenty years! Misreading my disbelief, she said, I know, I know, since the election they've cracked down on transplants for foreigners, but if your husband could just talk to my friend.

I agreed to speak to Oli. She thanked me profusely and said, Now, Ava, how are you? Tell me everything. It's been too long.

I ran through the checklist (while she pretended her private investigator hadn't already filled her in): Olivier, with whom she appeared to be already acquainted, husband of four years, half French, half American; Baby Henri, two years old—did she want to see a picture? Here he was in our backyard, yes, we lived right up the street.

And work?

I gave the stock answer: I'd left my law firm when Henri was born and was now considering going in-house, better work-life balance and all that. As I talked, I parsed her transformation. Eyelid surgery, of course, cutting-edge facials involving lasers and microcurrents, quality hair extensions, designer clothes. But it was more than that. Sitting across from me, sipping from that miniature ceramic cup, Winnie looked comfortable, relaxed; she looked like someone who belonged.

What had she done with the plump, earnest girl who'd entered our dorm room lugging a pair of scuffed hot-pink suitcases, filled, I would learn, with acrylic cardigans and ill-fitting polyester cuffed trousers? Right away, it'd been clear that we could not be friends.

Why, you ask? For all the usual superficial reasons that matter to teenagers. She was awkward, needy, fobby. No, f-o-b-b-y. Fresh off the boat.

Look, I wasn't cool then, either, but I wasn't a lost cause. I knew the right friends could buoy me and the wrong kind would sink me, and there was only a small window of time in that first year of college to get it right.

You see, Detective, it felt like I'd waited my whole life to get to Stanford. Growing up outside of Boston—Newton, to be exact, if you know the area—I was one of those quiet, nerdy kids everyone ignored. I mean, the teachers knew me because I had excellent grades, although they constantly confused me with Rosa Chee. She was my friend, along with all the other quiet nerds, but to the rest of the school, to the normal kids, I was invisible.

You want an example? One time my brother was home from college, and we went out for ice cream and ran into Mitch Paulson, his former tennis doubles partner. Gabe and Mitch slap palms, thump shoulders, and I kind of wave. I swear, Mitch's face goes completely blank. Gabe says, That's my sister, Ava, she's a junior, and Mitch says, perfectly pleasantly, Nice to meet you.

Nice to meet you! I'd watched at least a dozen of their matches. I knew who Mitch had dated all through his senior year, and who he'd dated before her. He had no clue who I was.

Stanford was full of kids like me. I had new contact lenses. I'd grown my hair long enough to braid. I was ready to be seen, and if I couldn't have a blond ponytailed jock roommate, I wasn't going to let the one I did have get in my way.

In my defense, I tried to be civil to Winnie. I squelched my impatience and answered her countless questions. Mostly basic things, like where to get a student ID and how to figure out her mailbox combination. But she also had this annoying habit of treating me like her pocket dictionary, asking me to define words she didn't know, and complicated ones, too: *doppelgänger, verisimilitude, conceit.*

Come to think of it, given that the vast majority of our interactions in college involved her asking for my help, perhaps I shouldn't have been so taken aback by this, her most recent request, to aid in arranging her friend's medical care.

Through the course of the afternoon, she disarmed me by commending my life choices, saying things like, It doesn't surprise me at all that you married someone both brilliant and handsome. And, I've always thought that half white, half Asian babies are the absolute cutest. And, Of all the girls at school, you're the one I envied most. Basking in her flattery, I failed to notice that she'd had me pegged from the start, while I'd completely misjudged her.

Winnie was feigning interest in the story of how Oli and I had met when an unmistakable cry pierced the air. I turned, along with Winnie and the other patrons. There, lying flat on his back on the sidewalk outside, his face a red ball of rage, was my Henri. Crouched beside him was Maria, bless her heart, talking quietly, a look of calm determination in her eyes.

For a split second, I considered claiming ignorance. (And before you accuse me of being heartless, Detective, you must understand that back then, the tantrums were never-ending.) At the next table over, two men in stylish glasses exchanged smirks, and I snapped out of it, explained to Winnie that the shrieking child was my son, and rushed out the door.

What happened? I asked Maria. I bent down to still my

son's wildly kicking legs. He cracked open one eye, saw it was me, and went right on wailing.

Maria sighed. Nothing, the usual, poor thing.

I stroked Henri's sweat-matted hair. Oh, Cookie, what's wrong? Tell Mama what's wrong.

But he couldn't tell me, and that was the root of the problem. Even at the age of two, he was deeply thoughtful, profoundly empathetic. More than anything he yearned to convey the feelings he had no language to describe, and who among us wouldn't find that frustrating? And so he erupted for the most innocuous reasons: being put in his stroller, being taken out of his stroller, having his hand grabbed before crossing the street, being toweled off after his bath. Anything could set him off. Those first few years, he cried so much, his voice was perpetually hoarse. Oh, but listen to me, going on and on about my happy, healthy kid. He's doing so much better now, even if he still sounds like a mini Rod Stewart. It's rather endearing, really.

That afternoon, however, my son went right on shrieking as Maria and I cycled through our repertoire of tricks, stroking his tummy, rubbing his scalp, tickling his forearms, pinning his ankles together. A woman walking a golden retriever clucked sympathetically at us. A nanny ordered a pair of twin boys to stop staring.

The only thing to do was to hunker down and wait it out, Maria and I making loud soothing sounds like a couple of white-noise machines. After a long while, Henri tired. His kicking grew less frantic; the muscles in his face slackened. I reached out and tickled his belly, which was sometimes enough to get him to relinquish the last of his rage. Not this time. The instant my finger poked his soft tummy, his jaw dropped, releasing a neck-pinching scream. The crying started up again at full force. I fell back on my haunches, exhausted, ready to tell Maria to peel him off the sidewalk and drag him home.

From behind me, a low, warm voice sang a Chinese children's song. Liang zhi lao hu, liang zhi lao hu, pao de kuai, pao de kuai.

I whirled around to find Winnie standing there bent over with her hands on her knees, singing intently about a pair of tigers, one without eyes and one without a tail. Zhen qi guai, zhen qi guai. I recognized the tune from the after-school Chinese classes of my youth.

Abruptly the crying stopped. Without breaking song, Winnie unclipped a gray fur charm dangling from the handle of her Birkin.

I blurted, Don't give it to him, you'll never get it back.

But she held the furry ball out to Henri in the palm of her hand.

I hope that's not real mink, I warned.

Henri seized the ball and squealed with delight. A thick rope of drool landed on the soft fur.

Oh dear, I said.

Winnie laughed and patted Henri's head, and he purred sweetly.

This is Auntie Winnie, I told him. Can you say thank you?

He rubbed the mink across his saliva-soaked lips.

I explained to Winnie that although he understood every-thing, he didn't yet speak, and Oli attributed the slight delay to his being bilingual.

Smart boy, said Winnie.

I was too embarrassed to go back inside the coffee shop, so when Maria managed to strap Henri into his stroller without incident, I suggested we head home.

There, Winnie settled at the grand piano and played "Twinkle Twinkle Little Star," singing to Henri in Mandarin—yi shan yi shan liang jing jing—teaching him to make blinking stars with his plump little paws.

The backs of my eyes began to smart. At that point my mom had only been gone six months. She was the one who was supposed to teach Henri Chinese. She was supposed to rub my back and tell me it was normal to be so tired I nodded off while brushing my teeth. She was supposed to talk me out of putting Henri on a strict diet of elk and ven-ison because I was convinced the hormones and antibiotics were to blame.

Winnie saw the tear winding down my cheek and lifted her hands from the keyboard.

What's wrong, Ava?

Henri tugged on his earlobe, signaling growing agitation.

Nothing. Keep playing.

She dropped her hands to her lap. Henri's wail started as a low, chesty rumble and then gained force, rising through the scale to full police siren.

Maria, I called.

She darted out of the kitchen, wiping her hands on the seat of her jeans, scooped up Henri, and hefted him to his bedroom.

I grabbed a tissue and dabbed my cheeks. Oli says it's a phase.

Sure, Winnie said. All babies are like that.

I didn't want her to think I was despairing over my son, so I told her about my mom's passing.

She clamped a hand over her mouth. She remembered my mom from when she'd visited Stanford all those years ago.

Oh, Ava, I'm so sorry. She must have been such a good grandma to Henri.

I told her that for the first three months, she, Henri, and I had shared a room. She woke for every feeding, changed countless diapers, promised me that someday he'd stop crying. She'd dropped dead—there was no other way to describe it—while jogging on her basement treadmill. Sudden cardiac arrest. Sixty-nine years old, thin as a whippet, rarely ever so much as caught a cold.

From the back of the house, my son's wails softened into jagged sobs. Winnie's mink charm lay gray and soggy on the carpet like an offering from a housecat. When I bent over to retrieve it, I caught the word *FENDI* embossed on the metal clip.

Oh, shit, I said.

Don't worry about it. Keep it as a toy for Henri.

Once she was gone, I searched for the bag charm online so I could buy her a replacement. Guess how much it cost? Six hundred bucks. Obviously I didn't go through with it. The next time Henri had an episode, I whipped out the mangled mink ball and dangled it in his face. He grew incensed, flung it away, and went right on screaming.

AFTER THAT, WINNIE WOULD LET me know whenever she came to San Francisco from L.A. Her work, she said, regularly brought her here, so she often stayed at the St. Regis downtown. I was impressed. The last time I'd checked, rooms there went for seven hundred a night.

Given all I've said so far, you must be wondering why I so willingly befriended her this time around. I'll admit that at first, I was dazzled by her wealth and beauty, her extreme confidence. I suppose a part of me was still stuck in freshman year, clinging to friends like life rafts.

But there was a deeper reason, too. The truth is, no one else, besides my mother, could calm Henri, and I was desperate. My son was still waking up every three or so hours, which meant it'd been two years and counting since I'd had a full night's sleep. Days I spent staring at my laptop screen, researching special diets to quell tantrums, while stalwart Maria wheeled Henri from story time to music class to the park. In fact, the week that Winnie called, I'd had eight pounds of bison shipped from Wisconsin, all of it hidden in a secret freezer in the garage storage room because Oli held a particular contempt for nutrition pseudoscience. And rightly so! I think we can all agree my behavior was unhinged.

Oh, and speaking of Oli, did I mention that this was right when he'd left UCSF for Stanford? A stellar career move, to be sure, but one that involved a nightmare commute on top of an already endless workday, which meant he never made it home in time to put Henri to bed.

So, like any overwhelmed new mom, I was grateful for Winnie's help.

Oli was glad to hear that Henri had taken to my old roommate, but was, like you, surprised at the extent to which I'd welcomed her into our lives. After all, the only thing I'd told him about Winnie was the infamous SAT scandal. I assume you've already been briefed?

No? Not at all? I see. I suppose that makes sense. I don't believe Stanford was officially implicated that time around.

This was back in the year 2000, and the whole thing was not unlike the recent incident with all those Hollywood bigwigs falsifying credentials and test results to get their kids into top schools, except, in this case, the perpetrators were Chinese nationals. According to the press, US law enforcement had uncovered a Beijing company that hired expert US-based test-taking proxies—Chinese grad students, mostly—armed them with fake passports, and sent them to sit for the SATs in place of wealthy, connected Chinese college applicants. Law enforcement seized company records and released their findings, and universities responded swiftly. Three Chinese students were expelled from Harvard, one from Yale, two from MIT, a handful of others from Penn and Columbia and Cornell. And you can bet that no one was writing op-eds in defense of these kids, portraying them as innocent victims who shouldn't be held responsible for their parents' crimes. No, when it came to foreign students, the universal rallying cry was to get those no-good Chinese cheaters out of our schools!

I remember standing by the fountain in White Plaza with kids from my humanities seminar, poring over fresh copies of the *Stanford Daily*. I returned to my room to find Winnie in tears, haphazardly chucking sweaters and T-shirts into her pink suitcases. She told me her father had a stroke. She was boarding a plane that night, never mind that finals started next week. I told her how sorry I was and folded my copy of the *Daily* into a tight square.

Did you tell your adviser? I asked. I was sure they'd let her make up exams.

She gathered an armload of socks and said, I really can't think about that right now.

I offered to notify her professors, and she smiled through her tears and thanked me.

The day of my last final, I received an email from Winnie. Her aunt was flying in from Virginia to pack the rest of her stuff. She was withdrawing from school. She didn't explain why.

Needless to say, everyone in the dorm speculated that Winnie had left just in time. Joanne Tran and Carla Cohen, who remain some of my closest friends, fixated on Winnie's less-than-perfect grammar. She mixed up *he* and *she*, forgot to add *s*'s to the ends of plural nouns, used present tense where it should have been past. Obviously, she couldn't have aced the verbal section of the SATs, much less written a personal statement that was up to snuff. They seemed to view Winnie's alleged cheating as a personal insult. Joanne pounded her fist against the flimsy dorm-room wall as she lamented having to take the test three times to raise her score, while those rich kids plunked down money for theirs.

I, too, was quite certain Winnie had cheated, and that she'd invented her father's stroke. But I wasn't angry. If anything, I felt sorry for her. Maybe because I'd seen how hard she worked; maybe because I knew she didn't come from wealth. Her parents weren't high-ranking officials like the parents of those Harvard kids. Her dad was a middle-school principal. Her mom, a secretary. She'd been able to enroll here only because she'd won a national government scholarship, plus her aunt in Virginia sent monthly checks. Even then, she worked the late-night shift at the coffee kiosk across from the library. She babysat and tutored. She chose her classes based on the number of required books. Whenever possible, she enrolled in the same classes I did so she could borrow mine. She'd set her alarm for the crack of dawn and finish her homework before I even awoke, never giving me reason to get annoyed and rescind the use of my books.

The day after I received Winnie's email, while Carla and Joanne and the rest of our floor chugged box wine to celebrate the end of the quarter, I hauled back boxes from the recycling bin behind the bookstore and packed the rest of Winnie's things. When her aunt and uncle showed up at our door, they were stunned by all I'd done. They took me out to dinner to thank me. But Winnie never thanked me. No doubt she had too much other stuff to worry about.

Did I ever confront her about the SATs? No, I didn't see the point. Why bring it up after all this time? She'd paid for her crime by leaving school, which is more than can be said for those Hollywood brats.

2

Before long Winnie was a fixture in our home. I must say her timing was uncanny. Somehow, she'd managed to resurface during the single most turbulent period of my life, and whenever something threatened to spiral out of control, there she was with a comforting word, a warm hug, a little present for Henri.

Once she brought over a beautifully illustrated children's book of Chinese folktales (tucked into another striking Birkin in peacock blue). I can honestly say I didn't recognize the little boy who climbed right into her lap to listen to the story of the Cowherd and the Weaving Maid. It was one that my mother had told me when I was a child, about a pair of star-crossed lovers who were tragically separated by the celestial river (that's the Milky Way, in case you were wondering).

The story was long and complex, much too mature for a child of Henri's age. After following along for a good while, he grew bored and seized a corner of the page. Winnie, though, had quick reflexes, and before he could rip the paper, she caught his wrist and said firmly in Mandarin, No.

I sprang up, ready to soothe my son, but, miraculously, no wails followed. Instead, he broke into a cheeky grin, squirmed down from Winnie's lap, and ran to the piano. He mashed his little fists into the quilted leather bench and gave her a beseeching look, making us roar with laughter. Maria murmured that perhaps he'd grow up to be a concert pianist, and I squeezed her hand, genuinely moved. It wasn't entirely far-fetched; Oli had exhibited real talent in his youth.

We spent the rest of the afternoon singing children's songs (while Henri stamped his feet and swayed with feeling), first in English and then in Mandarin, and then Maria taught us a few in Spanish, too. I was in the thick of the dreaded preschool application process—you know how it is, right, Detective? More competitive than the Ivy League? When Henri sidled right up to Winnie, laid his cheek on her lap, and sighed serenely, I could, for the first time, imagine him trooping off without us.

This Hallmark scene was what Oli walked into, a full hour before he was expected. He'd wrapped up early for once and rushed home to surprise me and take us out to dinner.

I introduced Winnie to my husband. She took his hand in both of hers and thanked him for fitting her ailing friend into his busy schedule. He patted her shoulder in an avuncular fashion and said, I'm happy to help.

Swiftly gathering her things, she made for the door, not wanting to intrude on our family time. As soon as she slipped on her shoes, however, Henri burst into tears. He lumbered over and fused himself to her leg.

I tried to pry him loose, saying, Auntie Winnie needs to get back to her hotel. She has to work. She'll visit again soon. To which Henri released a howl so anguished that Oli cut in with, Winnie, won't you join us? We're just grabbing pizza down the street.

She hesitated. I knew she was waiting for me to confirm Oli's invitation, but it had been so long since the three of us had gone out for a meal that I was torn.

Henri's howl climbed up a key; Oli pressed her again.

All right, she said. As long as I'm not intruding.

Of course not, I said at last.

Dinner proceeded as smoothly as it could have with a toddler at the table. Henri insisted on sitting next to Winnie and expressed his contentment by enthusiastically defacing his paper menu with green and purple crayons and then bestowing his masterpiece upon her. We scarfed down the pizza, scalding the roofs of our mouths with bubbling mozzarella. When Henri grew restless, I whipped out the iPad and headphones.

It was only after the plates had been cleared, the water glasses refilled one last time, and the check deposited beside Oli's elbow that he dabbed his napkin to his lips, cleared his throat, and delivered a piece of information so reprehensible,

I'd wonder if *he'd* in fact plotted to invite Winnie to dinner, knowing I'd be forced to temper my reaction.

Our conversation up to this point had been innocuous, veering from rising housing prices to worsening traffic, which had naturally led Oli to bemoan his terrible commute.

You know, he said. I may have found a solution.

Oh? said Winnie.

Oh? I said.

Apparently, one of Oli's colleagues had offered to rent him a small apartment on California Ave., ten minutes from the hospital. The place had been empty for months, so they'd given him a deal.

My smile strained the corners of my mouth. You're going to live in Palo Alto?

California Ave., that's a nice street, said Winnie.

Oli avoided my eyes. I thought we could give this a try. Only during the week. And when I have to work weekends.

Makes sense, Winnie said. What's that great brunch place with the very long queue?

Joanie's, said Oli, though I've heard the quality has deteriorated.

Does it make sense? I asked, still grinning like a buffoon. To leave your wife all alone with your active and fussy two-year-old?

Oli spoke slowly and calmly, like he did when he reprimanded said two-year-old. Come now, Ava. We discussed this before I took the job.

We discussed eventually moving *as a family*.

Yes, and what am I supposed to do in the meantime?

In the meantime, you make sacrifices because that's what's best *for the family*.

His expression grew plaintive. Why did you push me to say yes?

I swiveled to face him squarely so he could absorb my look of incredulity. Because it's your dream job. Because that's what good spouses do — support each other, help each other excel.

I said I was perfectly happy where I was.

I jerked my napkin from my lap and slammed it on the table. Winnie sucked in a breath. Even Henri glanced up from the iPad. The too-large headphones hung down to his jaw like Snoopy ears.

All right, I said. We can talk about this at home. I pushed back my chair, intentionally dragging its legs across the floor, savoring the deafening screech.

Oli tossed a bunch of twenties on the table, deftly pushing Winnie's hand away when she tried to add to the pile. Without warning he yanked Henri out of his high chair, and he promptly began to cry.

Outside the restaurant, Winnie stroked Henri's cheek, eliciting a despondent moan. She flagged down a cab idling nearby, and when she hugged me, she squeezed my shoulders and whispered, right in my ear, Call me.

Heat blazed across my face. I couldn't believe I'd let her witness this entire scene. Once she'd vanished, I raged at

Oli. Why did he have to get into this in front of my friend? How could he humiliate me like that?

He sputtered, I really didn't think you'd get so mad.

I whirled around and marched back to the house, leaving him to corral Henri and the stroller and the tote bag of toys.

I KNOW WHAT YOU'RE ABOUT to say, Detective. What was keeping me from packing up and moving down to the Peninsula with my husband? After all, I'm so eager to do so now.

One big reason was Maria. We'd gone through three other nannies before we'd found her, and I know it's cliché, but she really was part of the family. In the entire time she was with us, she only called in sick once—a vicious case of food poisoning—and I will never forget how Henri broke down when I told him she wasn't coming. He cried so hard, he started hyperventilating, his little chest pumping like the bellows of an accordion. I couldn't calm him down. I screamed into the phone at Oli that our son wouldn't stop, his lips were turning blue, he'd passed out. Infuriatingly composed, Oli told me not to panic and to call 911 if he didn't come to in another minute. Henri woke up right after that, but the terror's still fresh enough to send my pulse skyrocketing.

I thought of Maria as a true coparent. She was with me the afternoon my dad called to tell me about my mom. I couldn't comprehend what he was saying through the sobs. He repeated that she was dead and then abruptly hung up the phone to call my brother. When Maria entered the kitchen, she found me standing at the sink, the tap still running at full blast, bruising the sieve of strawberries. I asked her if it was possible that I'd misheard my dad. She bundled me in her strong sinewy arms and put me to bed and told me firmly that the only thing I had to do right then was grieve; she'd take care of everything else. Hours later, I gazed out the window into the backyard to see her kneeling beside Henri, their heads touching, and together they released a yellow balloon into the sky.

There was one other reason that prevented me from making the move: my foolish pride. Here, in San Francisco, surrounded by professional contacts and former colleagues, I was a lawyer on extended maternity leave, on *sabbatical* even—a concept that had, as of late, transcended the walls of academia and infiltrated corporate life. In the last couple of years, acquaintances had taken monthslong paid leaves to travel the world, volunteer at wildlife preserves, meditate in ashrams. Here in San Francisco, I could tell myself I wasn't so different from them.

Since my mom's passing, however, I'd grown increasingly certain I could never return to tax law and the tyranny of billable hours, a thought that so frightened me, I'd mentioned it to no one. You see, in my family there were only a few acceptable paths—law, medicine, engineering. Law was the one I'd disliked least. From the very beginning, I'd known my lot in life: to be good enough at my job, and to tolerate it until retirement.

This must sound so silly to you, Detective. Did you want to be in law enforcement ever since you were a little girl? Ah, your dad was a detective. I bet he told you that you could be anything you wanted, regardless of your gender.

I'm afraid I cannot fathom that level of freedom. Even at age thirty-seven, I was still obsessing over what my poor mother would have said if she'd lived to learn that I was becoming a yoga teacher or an interior designer or a baker—not that any of those things was my true passion, which only underscored the absurdity of my crisis. There wasn't anything else I wanted to do more!

So, what did I tell Oli? Absolutely nothing. I dreaded his disapproval most of all.

Here's a story that'll explain what I mean: Straight out of Berkeley Law, I joined a big firm and spent the year working almost exclusively with one awful partner. His name was Vince Garibaldi. Loud, sweaty, ruthless, a petty tyrant who chucked his blasted glass pyramid paperweight on the floor and called us motherfuckers when we messed up. I constantly feared getting fired.

When he wasn't yelling at me, Garibaldi loved to complain about his ex-wife. Like him, she'd been a successful lawyer, but she quit when they had their third child, and that, he asserted, was the beginning of the end. She went from being curious and opinionated to insular and dull. She couldn't carry a conversation that didn't revolve around something the kids said or did. Now, if he hadn't been my boss, I would have pointed out that he should have put more thought into who would care for their children before having so many. But part of me, I'm sorry to say, understood where he was coming from. At the time, Oli and I had just started dating, and I loved how well matched we were in every way—the same illustrious academic pedigrees, the same kind of prestigious, demanding jobs. A power couple in training. At his department holiday party that year, when his mentor asked how we were coping with Oli's grueling call schedule, he grinned with pride and said, Ava's hours are even worse than mine.

What would Oli think if I were to give up my career to, I don't know, write cookbooks? Following my husband to the Peninsula was one dangerous step closer to becoming a stay-at-home bore.

Now, looking back, I see all the things I got wrong, all my preconceived notions and mistaken assumptions. Yes, Maria is a stellar nanny, supremely competent and wholly caring, but I was so convinced of my own maternal shortcomings I placed her on a pedestal, certain she alone could ensure my son's well-being.

And in the same way I'd underestimated myself, I'd underestimated my husband. He wanted me to be a successful, high-powered lawyer because that's what I'd said I wanted. As you know, I've since come clean with him about, well, everything, and while he'll need time to digest it all, there's one thing I know for certain: whether or not I remain in law has zero bearing on where we go from here.

But I've gotten carried away. Enough about me. We're here to talk about Winnie.

3

Despite Winnie's urging, I didn't call her after that humiliating dinner. Instead, I wallowed in my misery, envisioning ever more dire scenarios. My imagination spun out of control. Far worse, I realized, than Oli embarking on an affair with some fresh-faced nurse was for him to figure out he didn't miss me at all, that he was perfectly content on his own.

I tried to put on a brave face. I threw myself into Henri's preschool applications, which were due that week. Over and over I explained why *this* preschool was a good choice for my child (and you know as well as I that *because it's walking distance from our house* wasn't going to cut it). I expounded upon my parenting philosophies, detailed hopes and dreams for my kid's early childhood education, unspooled a long list of his outstanding traits. *Classical piano music aficionado. Gentle and enthusiastic petter of neighborhood dogs.*

Nights I squeezed into Henri's new big-boy bed because it was the only way to get him to stop crying for his papa—and because, let's face it, it made me feel better, too. Countless times I composed the same message to Carla and Joanne but never went through with sending it. Even typing the words *I think Oli's leaving me* felt perilous, as though I could somehow write it into reality. In short, I was a total and absolute mess.

It was at this, my most vulnerable moment, that Winnie sensed a business opportunity. Until this point, her primary objective had been to secure Oli's aid for her ailing friend, Boss Mak. (Yes, everyone calls him that.) Now, however, sensing that she could take advantage of my fragile state (and my knowledge of tax law), she expanded her ambitions to recruit me into the fold.

That gray January morning, she called to see how I was holding up.

No, really, how are you? she asked, her voice thick with meaning.

The frayed cord within me snapped. Tears waterfalled from my eyes.

Ava? she said softly. Are you there?

I fought to steady my voice. Yes. A single syllable pinched so tightly, I gave up any hope of fooling her.

Are you okay?

No.

For a while she simply listened as I gulped air, trying to pull myself together.

Then she declared, He's going to hate living on his own so much, he won't last a month.

For some reason this made me laugh. I said, He signed a six-month lease.

Whatever. I still don't think he'll last more than a couple of weeks. Men are so helpless on their own.

He's wasting money we don't have.

The pause that followed told me this surprised her — transplant surgery is one of the highest-paid medical specialties — but we were still paying off grad school loans, the mortgage, Maria.

I added, But what can I say? I don't make a penny.

This, I believe, is when Winnie saw her opening. She announced she was taking me to lunch. Naturally, I said I didn't feel up to it, but she insisted nonetheless.

THE ROTUNDA, THE RESTAURANT ON the top floor of Neiman Marcus, was packed with tourists in designer sneakers, barricaded into their chairs by shopping bags, and ladies of leisure, checking their lipstick in tiny, gilded compacts. Winnie had yet to arrive. I was seated at a small round table next to a white woman who must have been in her eighties. The platinum bob, thick makeup, and nubby Chanel tweed couldn't mask her wizened form. She sat alone before a plate of crudité and a martini, and all the strapping, bronzed waiters addressed her by name. From the way she flirted with them, I could tell she'd been a beauty once. I watched mesmerized as she cut a small square of celery, dipped it into a ramekin of ranch dressing, and chewed as though it were filet mignon.

Winnie arrived with her peacock-blue Birkin in one hand and a large silver shopping bag in the other—something she had to return, she said.

We nibbled oven-warm popovers while waiting for our chopped salads.

Winnie took a sip of ice water and said, A little independence in a marriage isn't necessarily a bad thing.

I fiddled with the heavy silverware. It is when the independence only applies to one of you.

She lowered her voice. Do you have your own bank account?

My fingers jerked involuntarily, clanging my knife against my bread plate. What? We're nowhere near that point.

Right, she said quickly. Of course not.

Our salads arrived, and I changed the subject. What are you returning?

Oh, this. She glanced down at her shopping bag. A Celine purse I really don't need.

I gave a low whistle and admitted that I'd never understood the appeal of such expensive handbags.

They're a waste of money, she cheerfully agreed. Ever since the global conglomerates bought up the heritage designer brands, prices rise and quality plummets.

So why do people keep paying?

The same reason your parents shelled out for Stanford when you could have gone to a state school.

I begged to differ. My undergraduate education had led me to a top law school and then to a top firm.

She kindly refrained from pointing out how long it had been since I'd practiced law. She said, The point is they're status symbols. A Harvard degree is not so different from a designer handbag. They both signal that you're part of the club, they open doors.

So what you're saying is we're all getting fleeced.

She shrugged. Some people really like clubs. She held up the shopping bag. But me? I'm returning this and taking a stand.

I shaped my hands into a bullhorn and aimed it around the airy dining room, saying, Attention, attention, shoppers of Neiman Marcus, you've all been duped, as Winnie teasingly rolled her eyes.

When the check came, she snatched it up.

Too loudly I said, Don't be ridiculous. I can afford a damn salad.

The old woman at the neighboring table peered at us over the rim of her martini glass.

Winnie asked gamely, Are you enjoying your lunch?

Oh, yes, the woman said. I've come here every Tuesday for the last fifteen years. She tried to smile but her chemically paralyzed facial muscles could only form a grimace. To Winnie she said, I've seen you here before. You must be a regular, too.

No, Winnie said, I don't live in San Francisco.

Oh, then I've mixed you up with someone else. There are so many Orientals around here, and they all spend, spend, spend. She looked pointedly at Winnie's Birkin.

I shrank into the banquette, horrified, but Winnie remained composed. She downed the last of her espresso and said, There are over a billion of us. We are everywhere. Have a nice day.

Tracing our way out of the restaurant, I shook my head at Winnie, still dumbstruck.

She said, Old people are racist. My parents say stuff like that all the time and they're much younger than her.

Her magnanimity made me seethe. Suddenly it was of paramount importance that Winnie take my side.

But that word she used—there's no excuse, I said. We're people, not rugs. And what gives her the right to judge how you spend your money? She knows nothing about you.

Winnie laughed. You Asian Americans are so sensitive. Us Chinese, we know the world looks down on us, but we don't care! It takes only a couple generations for nouveau riche to become old riche, am I right?

She stepped off the escalator and led the way to the handbag department, stopping at the cash wrap. She set her shopping bag on the glass countertop, and a petite white saleswoman with a pageboy haircut and crimson lips hurried over. Mrs. Lewis, you're back in town.

Clearly, she'd mistaken Winnie for some other rich *Oriental*, but instead of correcting her, Winnie said, Deidre, hi, I hoped you'd be in today. She pulled out a square mass

shrouded in a taupe dust bag emblazoned with the word
CELINE. She went on, My mother-in-law says the color is
too bright. She doesn't dare carry it.

I shot Winnie a quizzical look. She'd been divorced
for years and never mentioned her ex-husband, much less
her ex-mother-in-law. Did they really keep in touch? How
close would they have to be to warrant such an extravagant
gift? Winnie's placid expression revealed nothing.

Inside the dust bag was a boxy minimalist tote—the
Luggage Tote, I'd later learn—in royal blue, the pigment
so brilliant and saturated, it was like gazing at the sole
Technicolor object in an otherwise black-and-white world.
Winnie slid a receipt across the counter, and I squinted at
the numbers. Three thousand one hundred and forty-six
dollars.

Oh, that's a shame, the saleswoman said. But we knew
it was a risk.

I tried to convince her, Winnie said, turning her palms
skyward. Let's go ahead and exchange it for black.

Oh dear, said Deidre. Didn't I mention this? We're out
of black. The entire company is sold out.

Oh no, said Winnie.

I'm so sorry.

It's my fault.

I examined my friend's face, trying to parse the conversation's many twists and turns.

Well, said Winnie, I guess I'll have to return this.

Of course, my dear. Deidre typed rapidly into the cash

register and scanned the barcode on the tag. It all goes back onto your Amex.

Thank you, Winnie said, patting the saleswoman's sun-spotted hand.

Come back and see us soon.

Winnie turned and headed for the side exit. I followed close behind.

Lewis? I asked.

She answered, For a time.

And you buy your ex-mother-in-law superexpensive gifts?

It's better to have a story.

Better for what? What are you talking about?

Out on the sidewalk, Winnie stopped and backed up against a wall, tugging me along with her. When she next spoke, her voice was so quiet, the traffic nearly drowned her out. I leaned in until my hair brushed her lips.

Remember how I told you I'm in handbag manufacturing?

I nodded.

I work with a particular kind of handbag. Replica designer bags.

What does that mean? Knockoffs?

She motioned for me to hush and held up her Birkin. How much do you think this cost?

A pair of Asian teenage girls slowed and stared unabashedly at the bag. Winnie took my arm and pulled me around the corner into a small, dingy coffee shop.

How much? she asked again. She sat down at one of the greasy-looking tables, as far away as possible from the only other customer, an elderly man in a fedora, reading the paper.

I threw out a wildly improbable number. I don't know, ten grand?

Sure, she said. If I bought this at the Hermès store down the block, it would have been close to twelve, including tax. That is, if I could somehow convince them to sell me one—they claim they're never in stock.

Where'd you get it then?

She gave me a smile that hid her teeth, inviting me to run my fingers over the supple grained leather, the gleaming gold hardware inscribed with the words *Hermès-Paris*, the *Made in France* stamp, the tiny H-imprinted lock. She let me take in every detail before answering.

This is from Guangzhou, the replica designer bag capital of the world.

It looks very nice, I said, though back then I had no idea I was looking at the crème de la crème of replicas, what's known as a one-to-one bag. Better than super A and just-plain A. (Even the replica handbag industry suffers from grade inflation.)

I was losing patience. What does this have to do with Neiman Marcus?

There again was that enigmatic smile. What do you think?

I think you import fake bags from China and sell them for a profit.

She grunted in disgust. Every Tom, Dick, and Henry does that. Where's the creativity? Where's the innovation?

I didn't bother correcting her. So tell me your brilliant business model.

Her eyes flashed like my son's did when he was about to dump his cereal bowl on the floor. What did I do in there? She pointed her thumb in the general direction of the department store. Didn't you watch the entire thing?

And then, it hit me. That gorgeous royal-blue bag was a fake. She'd returned a knockoff to the most exclusive department store in the world and pocketed the three thousand–plus dollars.

What did you do with the real one?

Sold it on eBay last week.

How did I react? I was furious. Much more so than I would have guessed. My whole body burned. My pores oozed sweat. I couldn't stand to look at Winnie's smooth white face. All at once, I understood how Joanne must have felt back in freshman year, punching the wall and cursing the injustice of it all.

I sputtered something like, But that's cheating!

Winnie was unperturbed. What about selling a bag for ten times what it costs to make. Is that not cheating?

Not at all. No one's holding a gun to your head forcing you to buy it.

What about manufacturing an entire bag in China, except for the handle, and then embossing the handle with a prominent *Made in Italy*?

What do you mean? That's neither here nor there.

What about forcing workers to go hours without bathroom breaks? Squeezing them for every cent and then turning around and selling their handiwork for thousands?

What are you trying to say? Many people do terrible things, that still doesn't make what you're doing okay.

She said, I'm merely suggesting that all of us fixate on certain kinds of cheating, while willfully ignoring other kinds.

A young man in a soiled apron sidled up and said, I'm sorry, tables are only for customers.

I'll take a double espresso, said Winnie, at the same time as I said, Don't worry, I'm leaving.

Confused, he backed away.

Ava, don't go, Winnie said. Those luxury brands, they're the villains. We're on the same side here. She pinned down my hand like she had the saleswoman's, as though she'd read in some manual that a firm touch at the right moment could weaken a person's resolve.

You're disgusting, I said before charging out the door.

Why did her admission infuriate me so? Why had I bothered trying to reason with her? We'd only just reconnected, and I owed her nothing. And yet, as I sped down the sidewalk, the conversation continued in my head, our respective retorts piling up like a tower of Jenga blocks.

And what disturbed me more was her utter lack of shame, her certainty that I would be receptive to her message.

In hindsight I see it was all part of her strategy: in hiding nothing, she forced me to consider the possibility that she had nothing to hide.

I met my Lyft at the end of the block. Safely ensconced in the back seat, I dropped my head and massaged my aching temples.

The driver called out, Temperature okay back there? A gold ring pierced her dainty snub nose.

Yup.

She turned up the volume on the stereo and a decade-old pop ballad filled the car. She sang along in a sweet, breathy voice. I keep bleeding, keep, keep bleeding love. She eyed me in the rearview mirror. I love this song.

I'd always thought the lyrics were "keep breathing, keep, keep breathing," and I told her so.

I keep breathing love? What does that even mean?

I gazed out the window. An ancient stooped Chinese woman inched a shopping cart of flattened cardboard boxes into the crosswalk.

Nothing, I said. It makes absolutely no sense.

4

We made a deal, you and I, and rest assured, Detective, I will tell you everything I know. But no matter how many times you rephrase the question, my answer is never going to change. I have no idea where she is. Her WhatsApp and email accounts have gone dark. Her phone number's been disconnected. And like I've already said, you can forget about social media—she guarded her privacy like the Sphinx. I imagine she's landed in one of those countries that doesn't extradite to the US—Morocco, or Indonesia, or Qatar. Isn't that what you'd do in her place?

Winnie didn't have many friends, here or back home in China. She had plenty of business associates and a few former lovers, and, of course, she had Mak Yiu Fai—Boss Mak—who had belonged to all three of those categories at various points in time. As you no doubt know, Boss Mak owns one of the most highly regarded handbag manufacturing operations in all of Guangdong. His factories' quality workmanship has earned him contracts with all the big designer brands that go to extreme lengths to hide the fact they manufacture in China: your Pradas and Guccis and Louis Vuittons. (An increasingly meaningless deception, by the way—there are as many sweatshops in Italy as there are state-of-the-art facilities in China.)

Winnie told me that she'd met Boss Mak in Shenzhen, completely by chance, when she was vacationing with her cousin and a few of her cousin's friends. This was three years ago, right after the 2016 election, which pushed her to contemplate moving back to China. By then she'd married, earned her green card, and divorced, and said that if she was going to live under an autocrat, it might as well be her own.

After a long day of shopping, Winnie and the group splurged on a meal at a restaurant in one of the big international hotels. That's when Boss Mak walked in alone. Tall and trim, with a full head of silver hair and a well-groomed mustache, clad in a slim-cut linen suit, he struck Winnie as the height of sophistication. He was sixty-seven—the same age as my mother, two years older than hers.

The hostess seated Boss Mak at the neighboring table, and he didn't balk, even though it was clear that the women were in a rowdy, celebratory mood. They'd spread out their purchases among the used plates: Louis Vuitton Neverfulls and Goyard PMs and Chanel flap bags—all fake, of course. That had been the whole purpose of the getaway. Winnie was the only one who hadn't bought anything. In fact, she told me she'd come along simply to escape her parents' claustrophobic apartment.

She happened to be seated nearest to Boss Mak, close enough to observe his skillful wielding of knife and fork as he cut his pork chop, the genteel way he chewed with his mouth closed between sips of Japanese whiskey.

When Boss Mak noticed her watching him, he asked what she'd scored at the shops that day.

Nothing, she said. She held up the tote she always carried, made from sturdy black nylon, purchased on sale at Macy's, and added, A bag is a bag is a bag.

That's the thing about Winnie: she didn't buy into the hype. She couldn't care less about fashion and status. When she got into the counterfeits game, she carried those absurdly expensive purses and donned those flashy jewels the way a flight attendant dutifully pulls on flesh-toned stockings. It was simply part of the uniform, and she'd do anything to maximize profits. This singular focus and pragmatism is what made her so successful.

That evening at the restaurant, Boss Mak picked up the tab for Winnie's whole table. One of the women announced they were going to a nearby KTV lounge and invited him along. He declined, and Winnie did, too, and the cousin and her friends, all of them married or at least engaged, traded knowing smiles and set off without them. Boss Mak and Winnie retired to the hotel bar and then to his suite.

Three days later, when she was back in Xiamen, a courier arrived at her parents' apartment with a stiff orange shopping bag, large enough to hide a puppy. Inside was a one-to-one replica Birkin 25 in cherry-blossom pink, along with a handwritten card:

A bag is a bag is a bag, but only a Birkin is a Birkin.
(Don't worry, this is a replica. I'm not that senseless.)

The note was clever, but the gift, in its excessive femininity and sheer frivolousness, made Winnie recoil. Later, she would tell me that trip to Shenzhen had given her a window into her future back home, and she'd abhorred what she'd seen. When I pushed her to elaborate, she explained that she had nothing in common with her cousin and those women. Oh, they were perfectly pleasant, but all they really cared about was making enough money to buy designer clothes and eventually send their kids to top universities. And the men were even worse.

But you and Boss Mak had a real connection, I said.

Precisely! she replied. That's all I had to look forward to—becoming the mistress of an old married man. Plus, I could tell right away he was a drunk.

(Over the course of their night together, he'd methodically emptied the minibar.)

Setting aside the fake Birkin, Winnie made up her mind right then and there to remain in the US. She bought a one-way ticket to LAX, determined to build a new life far away from Charlottesville, Virginia, and her ex-husband Bertrand Lewis. (Yes, the very same man who'd been married to her late aunt, but that's a whole other story, Detective. I'll get to that.)

Winnie knew she'd have to be careful with money in an expensive city like L.A. She moved into a studio apartment in a weathered building filled with college kids and bought a used Kia Sportage that rattled like a tin can on the freeway. Armed with a falsified résumé claiming she'd graduated from Stanford in 2004, along with the rest of us, she assumed finding an entry-level job in marketing or communications or sales would be straightforward. She sent her résumé to twenty-two companies and didn't land a single interview, so she widened her net, applying for Chinese-language teaching positions. She even attempted to get hired as a nanny after a Shanghainese girl pushing a double stroller revealed how much she was paid. When nothing panned out, Winnie started to panic.

One day, several months after her arrival, she happened to drive by a pawnshop, incongruously located a few blocks from Rodeo Drive. BEVERLY LOAN COMPANY read the sign above the dark-green awning, as intimidatingly elegant as that of any designer boutique. Her gaze fell on Boss Mak's rose-sakura replica Birkin in the passenger seat. Even without the original box and dust bag, she left with a check that would easily cover that month's rent, and, more importantly, the seeds of a new venture. Back at her apartment, she called Boss Mak for advice. He loved the idea so much he offered to cover her start-up costs. That's how he became the first investor in her business.

The very next day, an exclusive Chinese immersion school in Culver City called to offer her a job as a kindergarten teacher. Figuring she should hedge her bets, Winnie accepted at once.

IN THE BEGINNING, HERS WAS a one-woman operation. She opened a slew of credit cards under slightly different names to spread out her purchases and subsequent returns: Winnie Fang Lewis, Winnie Wenyi Fang, Winnie WY Lewis. And then she went shopping. At Neiman's, Saks, Nordstrom, Bloomingdale's, she started with a classic workhorse bag, the Longchamp Le Pliage. You know the one I'm talking about? I'm certain you'd recognize it. It's that rather flimsy nylon tote that folds up into a little square. Comes in just about every color you can think of, from violet to avocado to peach, and scarily trivial to copy. In fact, if you stand outside on the street for about an hour, I bet a half dozen of them, real and fake, would pass you by. Those early days, Winnie moved through so many of those bags she set up monthly shipments from China, certain she'd put them all to use.

From Longchamp she moved on to the long-standing Louis Vuitton monogram canvas styles, your Speedys and Noés and Almas. And then on to Prada, Gucci, Chanel, Dior. Within a year she'd amassed a small army of shoppers who surged across the country, snapping up luxury handbags as though they were socks.

You already know where she found these young Asian women—online, in those forums for bag fanatics, and then through personal referrals, always careful to hide her identity.

The work was more grueling than it sounds. She flew back and forth between Guangzhou and Los Angeles, personally vetting every unit, haggling for every cent. After she'd conquered the classic styles, she branched into the more exclusive, and therefore more lucrative, seasonal, and even limited-edition purses, which required a whole different tier of supplier.

And then, a year and a half into her life as an international businesswoman, with monthly revenue clearing a hundred grand, her application for American citizenship was accepted, grounding her in the US until the requisite interviews and appointments were completed. Again, she leaned on Boss Mak. With his extensive network of contacts, he could easily seek out quality counterfeits manufacturers and cement new relationships, and he likely would have done it for free if Winnie hadn't insisted on paying him a small commission.

This arrangement worked well until the day he showed up to a meeting slurring his speech and thoroughly confused about where he was. He was taken to the hospital, where his wife would tell the doctor that in hindsight, the whites of her husband's eyes had been yellowish for weeks.

For ten days, Winnie could not get a hold of Boss Mak. Her shipment was delayed, causing her to miss return deadlines for several high-priced handbags, slashing her profits. All would be forgiven when she learned Boss Mak had been hospitalized for liver failure, but that didn't make her troubles disappear. Without a trustworthy local contact, she had to do everything remote, studying high-resolution photographs from all angles, taking phone calls late into the night. But no matter how tirelessly she worked, the quality of the bags that arrived deteriorated, even from formerly dependable suppliers, and the prices continued to inch up. It was clear that if she didn't find an emissary to send to Guangzhou on her behalf, she would have to shut the whole thing down, perhaps even return to teaching those bilingual brats. (Her words, not mine.)

By the time she showed up at my neighborhood coffee shop, her desperation had reached Burj Khalifa heights. So imagine her amazement and delight upon discovering that I might in fact be the solution to *both* her problems.

SEVERAL DAYS AFTER THE NEIMAN'S fiasco, Winnie called me to apologize. She said she hadn't been thinking straight. Dealing with Guangzhou remotely was such a colossal headache that the stress had gotten to her. She was about to pay top dollar for a shipment practically sight unseen — she cut herself off then. You've made your views clear, she said, so that's the last thing I'll say about work. But, Ava, I want you to know that I've loved spending time with you and Henri. I hope we can remain friends.

I was still mad, and I told her so. She said she understood and wouldn't bother me again.

How I wish this were the end of the story. How I wish I'd ended that conversation and let her vanish from my life.

Maybe if I hadn't been so anxious about my marriage, my child, my flailing career—or if she'd showed up at any other time—I would have acted differently.

Imagine me standing there, phone in hand, taut with anger. Imagine my husband walking into the room. Imagine me throwing my arms around him, pressing my forehead to his.

You'll never guess what happened, I'd say. Can you believe she thought I'd be okay with what she did for work?

But these were not normal times. Oli didn't come home that night or the next. His text messages, when he sent them, were brief, and when I tried to video call him with Henri, right before bedtime, he was still at the hospital and answered only to say, Can't talk now. Love you, Son. Don't cry, I'm sorry, I have to go.

As my child worked his way into the fourth tantrum of the day, I fell back onto his bed, so broken I swear I managed to doze off amid his earsplitting screams. For an instant his cries faded into a roar of white noise, and then he hiccupped loudly. My eyes popped open. I cuddled and rocked him, and reasoned and pleaded with him, until he cried himself to the point of exhaustion and dropped into a deep slumber.

I dragged my aching body to my room, hot with fury. I hated Oli for having places to go, issues to contemplate, tasks to complete. He'd entrapped me in this house with a demon child. At that moment, the only thing that mattered to me was getting back at my husband. I wanted to make him feel as abandoned and powerless as I felt, to show him what it was like to be the one left behind.

I opened my laptop and searched flights to Boston to see my dad, Chicago to see Gabe. Without my mom around to corral us, seven months had passed since we'd all been together the week of her funeral.

But when I imagined confiding in my dad about my marriage, I saw the panic ripple across his face. If you're dissatisfied, tell him, he'd say, eyes shifting behind his glasses. Maybe he just doesn't know. And if I pushed him—Oh, I'm pretty sure Oli knows—he'd continue to re-treat, waving platitudes like a white flag: I'm sure you can work things out. When there's a will, there's a way. Every-thing will turn out fine.

And if you can believe it, telling my brother would have been worse. Laid-back, always in a good mood, Gabe would shrug as though I were the one overreacting and say, All you have to do is decide whether you want to move to Palo Alto, right? No need to make the problem any bigger than it is. I'd reply, Oh, is *that* it? Thank you for enlightening me, o wise one. To which he'd hold up his hands and tell me to simmer down, which would only rile me up more, and the cycle would repeat until I finally huffed away, enraged.

You wonder what my mother would have said? To be honest, I don't think I'd have dared tell her. Or rather, I would have downplayed our issues, pretended to support my husband's plan. Why? Because while she was never outwardly mean to Oli—she was too kind, too polite for that—she'd always held him at arm's length, wary of his charisma. She's the only person I know who didn't instantly succumb to my husband's charms. Perhaps that's why I got along with her best. The boundaries between us were finite and clear, and we couldn't argue about the things I didn't tell her.

At the top of my screen a banner flashed, advertising discounted tickets to Hong Kong. Aunt Lydia, Mom's older sister, had flown across the Atlantic for the funeral and planted herself by my side, her firm, cool hand on my back, steering me this way and that. Whenever I was cornered by one of Mom's colleagues or neighbors, my aunt fielded their questions, accepted their condolences on my behalf, and sometimes simply led me away. Before she left, she'd made me promise to bring Henri to Hong Kong to see my grandmother while she was still lucid, and I'd nodded dumbly, unable to conceive of how it was that I still had my grandmother while my baby no longer had his.

In my darkened bedroom, lit only by the glow of my laptop, I convinced myself this was the perfect time to take Henri to visit my extended family. After all, in a couple of months he'd start preschool and I'd find my way back to work in some capacity. The thirteen-hour flight would be challenging, of course, and I seriously considered asking Maria to come along. Only the thought of having to explain to my aunt and uncle that I couldn't manage my son on my own swayed me otherwise.

Before I could talk myself out of it, I entered my credit card information and hit purchase. I can honestly say it didn't cross my mind—that Guangzhou's right over the border from Hong Kong. You need to remember, back then I only possessed the sketchiest outline of what it was Winnie actually did.

5

Determined not to let Oli talk me out of this trip, I waited
twenty-four hours, until the cancellation window had closed,
to text him the details.

It was almost midnight. Still, he called me at once.

What? How? You can't take Henri.

The more frantic he grew, the cooler I remained. It's all
in the text.

Why didn't you tell me?

I burrowed beneath the covers with the phone pressed
to my ear. I just did.

Why now? All of a sudden? Let's go in a few months,
together. Let's take a nice vacation.

At that, I had to stop myself from throwing my
phone across the room. Come on, Oli, you never have
time.

You can't make such a long trip with Henri on your own.

I couldn't resist. I said, I've had a lot of practice lately,
managing on my own.

In the prolonged silence I sensed him beating back his

frustration. Finally, he said, Why are you so mad at me all the time?

Already he was paying more attention to me than he had in weeks.

I said, It's eleven days. You'll barely notice we're gone.

I heard his fist connect with a hard surface—the wall or table or nightstand—and I jumped. He wasn't the type who lashed out.

Ava, I should have handled this apartment thing better. I'm sorry. Please don't go.

Something in my chest thawed, but it was too late to change course. I said, It's a week and a half. Why are you making this such a big deal?

In a strangled voice he said, I work all the time. I'm not down here hanging out and having fun.

Powerless against what I'd set in motion, I barreled ahead. Then you'll get plenty done without us interrupting you.

He sharpened his tone. We both know you won't even survive the flight out.

AND, WELL, OLI WAS NOT wrong about that. At first Henri charmed the flight attendants, waving his fat little paws and beaming whenever they came down the aisle. I smacked my lips against his cheek to make him squeal, hoping against reason that we'd left behind the terrible twos and entered a new and glorious phase.

His good mood soured when I strapped him into his

car seat for takeoff. He wept when the plane lifted into the sky and when I changed him and when I tried to feed him applesauce from the kids' meal. (By then I'd given up on bison, and I'd suspended his low-glycemic diet for the duration of the trip.) He wept when I carried him up and down the aisle, up and down, up and down, because I didn't know what else to do. At first, I locked eyes with every passenger to convey how deeply sorry I was, but after the fourth glower, I trained my gaze straight down at the dark carpeting, singing softly, futilely into Henri's ear. Even the nicest of the flight attendants, who, for the first few hours, had smiled sympathetically and offered little sweets and toys, turned on us, snapping at me to stop blocking the bathroom door.

You mentioned your two girls, Detective. How old did you say they were? So you remember how it was when they were little. Oli says Henri has unusually sensitive ears—his eustachian tube and all that—which makes flying especially uncomfortable, poor thing. It's supposed to be something he'll outgrow.

All the way to Hong Kong Henri wailed in delirium, fighting off sleep. The instant we boarded a cab to my aunt's, he dozed off. I took pains not to jostle the stroller as I wheeled him into the elevator, leaving our luggage in the lobby, relieved that at least my family wouldn't be greeted by a bawling, inconsolable child.

I tucked Henri into bed while my uncle went down to retrieve our bags. Then I joined the grown-ups in the living room. The balcony looked out onto a forest of pale, tightly wedged apartment towers, bathed in late-afternoon sunlight. I snapped a picture and posted it online with the caption, *Made it!*, hoping to provoke Oli.

My aunt and uncle's cozy flat was on the fifteenth floor of an old but well-maintained building in Happy Valley. My aunt had always loved to draw, and her oversized pastels of her daughters and granddaughters filled the walls. Aunt Lydia told me that my grandmother, whose assisted living facility was not far away, had been asking for me all week. Uncle Mark said that my cousins sent their love. (Kayla was a pastry chef at the Mandarin Oriental; Karina, an ophthalmologist who'd recently relocated to Singapore.) My aunt and uncle nodded approvingly when I mentioned Oli's new position at Stanford, and I recalled that Karina's orthodontist husband had left her for his assistant, which had precipitated her move abroad. I told them that Gabe and his wife were newly pregnant, and when my aunt smiled, a dimple pulsed in her right cheek, just like my mom.

All over Hong Kong I'd see people who looked like they could be my relatives—the same broad cheekbones, high foreheads, tanned skin. The first time I'd come here at age three, how stunned I'd been to see all the Chinese people milling about the airport. Everyone looks like us! I'd exclaimed to my mom and dad, who'd laughed loud enough to draw stares.

It was nearing dinnertime when whimpers rose from the guestroom. I hurried to Henri's side, pulled up *Thomas the Tank Engine* on the iPad, and, once his eyes had glazed over, jumped in the shower. The next time I checked my phone, there was a long series of messages from Winnie:

Hey, I hate how things ended btw us. I'm sorry again for making you feel so uncomfortable.

Not making excuses. Just want to explain I'm under a lot of pressure trying to deal with this Guangzhou shipment and wasn't thinking straight. I'm sorry I put that on you.

Anyway you're in Hong Kong?! Visiting family? Have an amazing trip. Hope we can see each other when you return!!

It didn't occur to me then, but now, looking back, I see that of course she was monitoring my social media posts even though she claimed not to have accounts of her own. I tossed my phone aside and rooted around in my suitcase for one of the new toys I'd stashed. Waving a miniature airplane at Henri, I slid the iPad into a drawer before carrying him outside. For the next few minutes, Aunt Lydia and Uncle Mark mussed his hair and stroked his cheeks and praised everything from his long eyelashes to his large-for-his-age feet, while I stood with my hands clenched, willing my son not to break down. Miracle of miracles, he demoed his airplane, flying it high above his head and zooming enthusiastically. I kissed his temple, proud.

We managed to reach my aunt's chosen restaurant with minimal tears. There, we feasted on smoked duck and crispy salt-and-pepper shrimp, and I guzzled down strong jasmine tea to fend off drowsiness.

Once the complimentary bowls of mango pudding had been set on the table, I whipped out my credit card like a cowboy pulling a pistol and triumphantly thrust it at the waiter. My aunt and uncle protested wildly, causing Henri to holler with glee, but I held my ground.

Within minutes the waiter returned and stooped to mutter that my card had been declined. Again, my uncle reached for his wallet. I shoved my debit card at the waiter and blathered about how I'd forgotten to notify my bank about the trip.

Don't be silly, Ava, my aunt said. Let us pay. You can sort things out with your bank later.

American kids are like this — so independent, said my uncle. Our kids never try to pay!

We're so grateful to be staying with you, I said.

My aunt said, Nonsense, you're family.

The waiter came back, his regretful hunch signaling that this card had also been declined.

Your bank has good security, Aunt Lydia said as my uncle handed over his card.

I was so embarrassed that when Henri managed to seize one of my chopsticks, I almost welcomed the distraction. I snatched the utensil from his grasp, accidentally poking him in the cheek, which gave rise to indignant shrieks. I jumped up and bounced him in my arms, chanting apologies to him and everyone else within earshot.

Once Uncle Mark had signed the receipt, we hustled out the door.

Back in the flat, I set Henri before the iPad and called my bank, still feeling more irritated than worried. A cheerful woman with a South Asian accent answered my call, assuring me that she'd do her best to resolve my problem if I wouldn't mind holding. Classical violin music filled my ear.

Ms. Desjardins? The woman pronounced it "Dess-jar-dinns." I was used to it.

Wong is fine, I said.

Pardon?

Wong. Ms. Wong.

Oh, right, sorry, Ms. Wong-Dessjardinns. I believe I've figured out the problem.

Great, so I can use my card now? I glanced over at Henri, who'd fallen asleep in child's pose, as though he'd been begging for something on his knees and suddenly plunged face-first into slumber.

No, I'm afraid not. It's a bit more complicated than that.

What is it? The question spilled from my mouth, leaving behind the bitter aftertaste of dread.

The woman spoke carefully. It appears that Mr. Dess-jar-dinns has removed you as an authorized user of his credit cards.

What does that mean?

It means your credit card no longer works.

I slapped my thigh so hard I winced. Henri didn't stir.

It appears he also changed the settings of your joint account so that both of you, together, must approve all future withdrawals.

So I can't use my debit card, either?

Not if he doesn't approve the transaction.

When did he do this? Why wasn't I notified?

January twenty-third, so, yesterday.

I charged into the bathroom and shut the door. You don't understand. I'm in Hong Kong. I don't have any money.

I do apologize, but because the primary account holder is Mr. Dess-jar-dinns . . . her voice trailed off.

Deh-zhar-daaa, I snapped.

Pardon?

Nothing, sorry, forget it. What options do I have? I'm abroad, you see, and I have my baby here with me. Can you give me access until I can reach my husband?

In the same monotone the woman said, I do apologize, but I'm not permitted to do that.

My voice ricocheted off the bathroom tiles. How could he have done this without anyone notifying me?

I do apologize, but he's the primary account holder —

All right, all right, I get it. I ended the call and then dialed Oli's cell again and again.

His voice-mail message taunted me like an incessant advertising jingle. Hello! You've reached Dr. Olivier Desjardins. Please leave me a message and I'll get back to you shortly!

At last I gave up.

Obviously I wasn't in any real danger. My aunt and uncle would give us everything we needed—he knew that as well as I did. What he wanted was to shame me, to force me into confessing my sorry situation to my family.

And I can't say that I blame him. After all, he'd begged me not to go, and I hadn't listened, opting instead to attempt to outrun our problems like some reckless, angst-ridden juvenile.

You seem surprised, Detective. You probably think what he did was unacceptable, evidence of some deep misogynist streak, an obsessive need for control. That's the kind of knee-jerk reaction a lot of us feminists would have, but I can assure you that's not Oli. The truth is, I put him under a lot of pressure when I left my job, rendering us a single-income household. The baby had just been born and our expenses rose alarmingly. Henri couldn't have been more than a couple weeks old when sleep deprivation led me to make a slew of costly, careless errors—I missed a couple credit card payments and got slapped with a bunch of late fees; I wrecked my car's side mirror while backing out of the garage; I left the faucet on in the laundry room, which resulted in two grands' worth of water damage. After that, Oli took charge of our finances for a while, arranging for our bills to be sent to his email address. Honestly, it was a relief when he changed the structure of our bank account, demoting me from joint account holder to authorized user. It assuaged some of the guilt I felt for not working. And with my head and heart full of Henri, I was more than happy to relinquish responsibilities, especially if that lessened Oli's stress, too.

Oh, don't look at me like that. Surely by now you know I'm not some deluded housewife, content to perpetuate the patriarchy. My mom used to give me that same look, as if she could not quite believe she'd fought this hard for gender equality, only to watch her daughter give it all away. But that's the thing her generation doesn't understand. Equality is about having choices, even if my choice isn't the one she would have made.

You know, a couple of days before my wedding, she cornered me to ask about our finances. I remember being taken aback. She'd more or less left me alone to figure things out since I'd graduated college. I told her Oli and I had merged our accounts to have one less thing to worry about.

She hitched her lips to one side. It's not a bad idea to have some money of your own.

A giggle escaped me. What did she take us for—a helpless, financially dependent damsel and a boorish chauvinist? At the time my salary was three times his! When I saw she was serious, however, I gathered myself. I didn't know where to begin. I settled for explaining that California was a joint-property state. Say I were to stop working for a couple of years for whatever reason, and then Oli and I divorced, all assets accumulated over the course of the marriage would be divided straight down the middle. If anything, I joked, I should be making him sign a prenup, in case we split before he becomes an attending.

I heard the cockiness in my tone, and she did, too. Her mouth formed a grim line. She said, I know, I know, you went to the best schools. You have a fancy job. I'm just saying, think about it.

I did not.

Now, I chucked my useless plastic cards on the bath mat. During my last conversation with Oli, before I'd boarded the plane, he'd said, You can't have it both ways. You can't drop a couple grand whenever you feel like it and then get mad at me for working to earn that money.

I was so enraged, I couldn't speak. Our house, our rules, my parents had intoned variously throughout my teenage years. All that latent adolescent ire flared within me, and the only thing I could muster was a cold, Don't you dare, before ending the call.

There was no way I could let him win—not by apologizing and pleading for mercy, not by humiliating myself before my uncle and aunt. What can I say, Detective? You don't earn straight A's all your life without being uncommonly competitive.

I'm sorry, I don't mean to make light of what I've done. I was trying to explain how my almost pathological sense of drive kicked in, convincing me that only one option remained. I reached for my phone and typed a message to Winnie: There's a problem with my bank account and I need access to funds fast. Do you still need someone to go to Guangzhou?

Her reply came within seconds: Chat now?

I perched on the edge of the tub and waited for her

call. She didn't waste time with pleasantries. She told me to grab a pen and paper because she couldn't send anything in writing.

Telling myself there was still plenty of time to back out, I complied.

The following morning, she said, a driver would arrive at my aunt's flat to ferry me across the border to the Baiyun Leather World Trade Center, the world's largest retailer of replica designer leather goods.

Hang on, I said. I haven't agreed to anything yet. Is this place dangerous?

Ava, Winnie said, it's a regular mall.

There, at Baiyun, I'd find the store run by Winnie's contacts, where I'd inspect and pay for fifty Chanel Gabrielle Hoboes in all the latest colors and fabrics.

This, too, gave me pause. What the hell was a "Gabrielle Hobo"? What exactly was I supposed to inspect?

You can do this, she said firmly. Look at the bag from all angles. Smoosh the leather—it should be soft and pliable. Make sure the zippers pull smoothly, that the stitching is even, that the trims and seams line up. Check the hardware. Read every word on the authenticity card.

I scribbled notes as quickly as I could.

What if I can't tell the difference between a good and a bad fake?

Take pictures—close up, interior and exterior—and send them to me.

This final directive set me more at ease, but also

prompted me to ask why she couldn't handle all this from L.A.

Winnie let loose an exasperated exhale. Ava, we're not buying from some reputable name brand. These people are crooks. They could charge me for one-to-ones and ship me a bunch of crap. You're the only one I trust.

Hearing her refer to her own associates as crooks shook me from my trance. What was I thinking? I'd never done anything remotely illegal in my life, and the last thing I wanted was Winnie's trust.

No, I can't do this. I'm sorry for wasting your time.

Don't hang up.

The command immobilized me.

All I'm asking is that you show these people they're being watched. A favor for an old friend. You're not doing anything criminal. You're harming no one.

Again, I demurred.

She said, Look, I'm not going to ask why you suddenly need money, but if it's really as urgent as it seems, this is the easiest cash you'll ever make.

She told me that after I'd inspected and paid for the bags, they'd be sent on to Dubai, where they'd be split into small unremarkable parcels that would escape notice in the US.

Once she received the shipment confirmation, she'd send my commission.

I asked, Five percent of what? The cost price or the retail price?

Retail. I'm not a cheapskate.

I did the math. If each bag's real counterpart sold for four grand online, she'd earn double that amount after returning the fake to an unsuspecting department store.

When I pointed this out, she released a short bark of a laugh and said, Good point, good point. I should know better than to go up against a Stanford grad.

Before I knew it, we'd settled on doubling my commission, to be doled out in three installments.

I said, I still don't feel good about this.

Winnie's tone melted like butter on toast. You'll feel better once you see how smoothly everything goes—and once you get paid.

She advised me to open a mobile wallet on WeChat for convenience and privacy, pointedly refraining from asking what was going on with my bank account. (As you and I have already discussed, she had other ways of getting answers.)

I'll send all payments to your WeChat, she said. I heard the wink in her voice when she added, No one will ever need to know.

Winnie's driver arrived at seven o'clock sharp the next morning to make the two-hour journey to Guangzhou. Gathering my things, I stopped at the dining table, where Henri sat in between my uncle and my aunt, gnawing on cornflakes.

I bent to kiss him on both cheeks. Bye, Cooks, I said. Be a good boy.

He tossed a handful of cornflakes after me, as though they were grains of wedding rice. If I weren't in such a hurry, I might have been amused.

My aunt leapt up to gather the scattered cereal.

I rushed back to the table and smacked his hand. Cookie, we don't throw food. I bent down to help my aunt.

Henri giggled and tossed another handful right in my face. I grabbed his arm. No. We don't do that.

My uncle whisked the bowl away. You don't get to eat cereal if you throw it.

I'm so sorry, I said.

Neither my aunt nor my uncle responded, but I caught

the look that passed between them and guessed they already regretted their offer to watch Henri. My cell phone chimed—the driver making sure I knew he was here. Henri whimpered and tugged his ear.

Now, Cooks, no crying, I warned.

He slapped his high-chair tray, demanding more cereal.

I slowly backed toward the door, still clutching his discarded cornflakes in my fist. Don't. Cry.

His gaze locked onto mine.

Be. Good.

His eyes filmed over.

Go, said my aunt. Don't be late.

Have a good time with your friend, my uncle said.

That's what I'd told them—that I was going to meet an old law school classmate.

Thank you, I said. Really, thank you so much.

As I shut the door behind me, my son's whimper rose to a screech. I darted into the elevator and jammed the close button. All the way down, I stared up at the security camera, urging it to note the face of the world's worst mother. In the less than twenty-four hours we'd been in Hong Kong, my aunt and uncle had already endured one tantrum and were well into their second. I half expected them to tail me into the lobby, shouting that they'd changed their minds.

Have you taken him to a specialist? my aunt had asked gently the night before. I can get Karina's advice? I reminded her that his father happened to be a doctor, too, and she let the subject drop.

In the lobby, I deposited my child's cereal in the trash. Beyond the glass door stood my driver, a middle-aged man with a small paunch and thinning hair. It wasn't too late to cancel. I could empty my wallet of the last of my dollars and send him away with a simple apology. I could go upstairs to my crying boy.

And then what? How would I explain why I had no money? How could I reveal what my husband had done without raising alarms? Oh, how the family would pounce on the gossip. If my mother were still around, my aunt would have messaged her right away to make sure she knew, and my cousins, too. In fact, at this very moment, Aunt Lydia was probably calling Karina to report on Henri's *issues*, and to ask whether it'd be okay to give him a tiny bit of Benadryl to settle him down.

Later that night, as my aunt and uncle got ready for bed, she'd say, Can you believe that Oli? Jana told Ava to keep her own bank account, but she refused.

American kids, my uncle would say. So stubborn.

Perhaps they'd touch hands, secretly thankful that Karina wasn't the only one whose husband had proven to be a cad.

No, I could not reveal the truth. Letting down my guard seemed as unthinkable as stripping naked in my aunt and uncle's living room. And now I'd taken on the additional burden of not wanting to disappoint Winnie.

Maybe all this is difficult for you to understand, Detective, but when you grow up as I did, schooled in the

supremacy of "face"—the figurative face, the image, reputation, honor that must be fought for and preserved at all
costs—breaking free from constraints to think for oneself
becomes a Herculean task.

And so, I went outside, and greeted the driver, and
climbed into his minivan.

We wound our way through teeming city streets,
flanked by buildings packed so closely together they formed
an endless wall of gray. From time to time, the driver tried
to make conversation, but my Mandarin was limited to cursory discussions about food and the weather, and my Cantonese was worse. Eventually, he turned up the radio and
listened to the news.

I must have nodded off because the next time I checked,
we were careening through traffic on the wrong side of the
street. In crossing the border, it was as though we'd passed
through a mirror: everyone here drove on the right side of
the road, and we did, too, except that my driver was still
on the wrong end of his van. When he signaled and made
a sharp left turn, my stomach lurched. We were misfits, he
and I, aliens in this strange, exotic land.

My driver weaved in front of a lorry filled with wooden
crates of cawing chickens and pulled up to a peach-colored
tower, one of five that spanned an entire city block.

We're here.

Even though Winnie had given me a shop number,
#04-21, I'd somehow still expected an outdoor, sprawling
mass of stalls, like the night markets of Mong Kok and

Temple Street. But there was nothing temporary, nothing illicit about this shopping center where the world's best replica designer handbags were displayed and sold. Steps away from the entrance stood a makeshift police kiosk housed inside a trailer, further contributing to the surreal nature of this place, and of my impending assignment. How could I be about to commit a crime when the entire city seemed, blatantly and nonchalantly, to be doing the same?

A woman sidled up and snapped a flyer at me, Vegas-strip style. Handbags for a beauty like yourself? Designer handbags?

A young man in uniform emerged from the trailer and lit a cigarette.

No, thanks, I said.

Inside the mall, I peered into shop after tiny shop, ogling the handbags crammed onto shelves like grocery cans. These lower-tier stores stocked a hodgepodge of brands, a compilation of the luxury handbag industry's greatest hits: the Gucci Dionysus next to the Fendi Baguette next to the Louis Vuitton Speedy. The more upscale, higher-priced stores focused on single brands: Celine or Goyard or Issey Miyake's Bao Bao line in every style and color ever dreamed up.

The stores in the highest tier held prime locations right by the escalators. They were spacious and decorated with intention and had actual business names like Cherished Dreams Handbags and Revive the Nation Leather Goods. Taking their cues from real designer boutiques, they displayed each bag like a sculpture beneath a single spotlight. Even their sales staff was super-A quality. When I asked to take a closer look at a Chanel clutch on a high shelf, a lithe young woman, clad in a classic tweed jacket, thigh-high cap-toed boots, and a little newsboy cap adorned with interlocking C's, walked me through the replica's many virtues, from the buttery calfskin (imported from France) to the glistening gold-toned hardware.

Across the way, a gargantuan chartreuse Birkin the size of a bassinet lured me into an immaculate store that sold only Hermès. With its opulent Instagram-ready windows, featuring random accessories for the haute-bourgeois life of leisure—a backgammon set crafted entirely from untreated cowhide, a glossy horse saddle and matching riding crop— this store would not have been out of place on Madison Avenue or Rue Saint-Honoré. In addition to the sizable handbag section, a corner of the store was devoted to those iconic silk scarves, another to candy-colored enamel jew- elry, a third to riotously patterned dishware. I lifted a Kelly bag in a vivid amethyst shade off the shelf and turned it this way and that, as though I knew what to look for.

A sales associate dressed all in black except for an emerald-and-magenta silk triangle draped from her neck told me it was a brand-new fall color.

It's lovely, I admitted. How much?

I converted yuan to dollars in my head and was sure I'd done the math wrong, so I sheepishly tapped the numbers into my phone: fourteen hundred dollars.

How much did you say? I asked.

She repeated the number. It's a good deal.

Right, I said. I see. Winnie *had* said the real thing went for twelve grand, so, in a sense, the associate was right. I gingerly returned the bag to the shelf and left, still firmly under the belief that no handbag, real or fake, could possibly be worth that much.

No longer in the mood to explore, I went straight to the fourth floor to complete what I'd come to do. It was late morning and the mall bustled with wholesale shoppers wheeling oversized suitcases that would soon bulge with merchandise to be fanned out across shelves in Manila and Buenos Aires and Moscow.

Tucked away in the very back of the complex, #04-21 was modestly decorated and badly lit and had no sign above the entrance. (Winnie would later assure me that their workshop produced some of the most authentic-looking bags she'd ever come across, but they kept the good stuff hidden away whenever they were tipped off about a police raid.) I told the attendant, a model-thin young man with hollow cheeks, that I worked for Fang Wenyi, and he offered me a stool and a glass of hot tea before calling to check on my order.

It's ready, he announced, and then went back to tapping on his phone.

I looked around, wondering what I was supposed to do next—pick the bags right off the shelves? Was that the Gabrielle right there in the corner? Could I pull out my phone to discreetly compare it to the picture I'd saved earlier that morning?

An older man burst into the store. He was short and muscular, sporting fashionably ripped jeans and pristine white high-tops.

Nice to meet you, nice to meet you, come with me, he said without bothering to introduce himself.

I was confused. Where?

Now he was confused. Where? To get your bags.

Oh, I said. Good. Let's go.

He led me down a back staircase that reeked of cigarette smoke.

You're American? he asked, scanning me from head to toe.

Yes. That's why my Chinese is so bad.

He laughed. It's decent.

So where are we going? I asked.

He pointed into the indeterminate distance. Down the road.

He walked briskly, dodging motorcycles, ignoring traffic lights, and I fought to keep up, raising the palm of my hand to drivers in both a gesture of apology and a plea for them to brake before they hit me.

We passed another massive shopping center that specialized in the metal hardware that festooned bags and belts and shoes. I didn't dare ask my companion how these stores, all of which sold the same few items, could possibly survive side by side. That's how little I knew. It would take me a few more months to grasp the size and complexity of the counterfeit accessories trade.

The man turned down a narrow street and stopped in front of a shabby-looking apartment building.

Here? I asked. I'd expected a warehouse with security, maybe a receptionist.

He shot me a sidelong look. Yep. He pulled out a ring of keys and unlocked the front door.

I followed him down a darkened hallway, listening for any signs of life beyond the walls, sniffing the air for cooking smells. The building was eerily still. If, for some reason, I had to scream, would anyone come to my aid?

He stopped before the last door at the end, and I sized him up. He was only a couple of inches taller than me, but when he pushed open the door, his forearm flexed, displaying ropy muscles, bulging veins. He flicked on a light. A slim length of neon yellow glinted in his back pocket—a box cutter. I took a step back.

Hold on, I said, pulling out my phone and studying the blank screen. Sorry, I have to take this call.

He left the door ajar. I typed a message to Winnie: This man, older, short, muscular, wants me to go inside his apartment to get the bags. This can't be right? I stared at the screen, willing a response to appear. Who knew who else was inside that apartment, waiting for a naive American to stroll right through? I removed the money from my wallet—two measly twenties—and jammed them into my bra. I laced my house keys between my fingers and wondered if, when push came to shove, I'd really dare gouge out an eye. I checked my phone. No response.

The man's head popped out around the side of the door, startling me.

Ready?

What choice did I have? I stuffed my phone in my purse and went inside.

Bulging jumbo-size garbage bags filled the floor of the main room, which was unfurnished except for two plastic chairs and a plastic table with an overfilled ashtray, all pushed up against one wall. The door clicked shut, and I heard the man turn the lock. Sweat surged beneath my arms but my mouth went dry. Behind my back I clenched my fingers around my keys.

Want something to drink?

I stammered, No, thanks.

He picked his way to the kitchen and emerged with two green bottles of beer, one of which he held out to me. I shook my head, and he shrugged and deposited the spare on the plastic table. He pulled the box cutter from his pocket, extended the blade, and deftly popped off the bottle cap before taking a long swig.

I don't want to take up too much of your time, I said, speaking loudly to drown out my thrashing heartbeat.

He wiped his mouth with the back of his hand and pointed the blade in my direction. I sucked in a breath.

You and Fang Wenyi—how long have you been working together?

What was the right answer? I said, Only a short while, but we've known each other for twenty years.

She's very capable, he said, but it sounded like a question.

Yes, she seems to be good at her job.

He wagged the box cutter like a finger. Yes, too good.

I could not parse where this was going.

She got me in trouble with the big boss. He doesn't like the price she bargained me down to. Make sure she knows it's a onetime thing.

I'll pass on your message, I said. I don't make decisions, I follow instructions. I'm supposed to inspect the shipment now?

He stuck the box cutter in his back pocket, took another swig of beer, and belched softly.

So where are the bags? I asked. My keys tumbled onto the floor, and I bent to retrieve them.

He narrowed his eyes. Why so antsy? You're in a rush?

The lie gushed out of me. Yes, actually. My family is here in Guangzhou. I'm meeting them for lunch, my husband and son.

Your husband, he's American?

I knew what he meant. Yes.

What does he do?

He's a surgeon.

How old is your son?

Twelve, I said, and then wondered why I'd bothered. I pictured Oli and my imaginary twelve-year-old crashing through the door to rescue me.

The man closed the distance between us, and like one giant muscle my entire body tensed. When his hand went for his back pocket, a cry rose in my throat.

He pulled out his phone. My son's ten, he said. Almost as big as yours. He thumbed the screen and offered an image of a chubby boy spinning a basketball on one finger.

I could have collapsed onto the heap of garbage bags in relief. Very handsome, I said.

Show me yours.

I told him I didn't have any pictures, and he looked incredulous.

It's a new phone, I lied.

All right, all right, you're in a hurry. He checked the notecards stapled to a trio of garbage bags in one corner. Here they are.

I knelt down and opened the first bag. The new-car smell hit me in the face. I inspected the tricolored chain straps, tested the zippers on the interior pockets, took pictures of each colorway from multiple angles.

The man watched, amused. Fang Wenyi must not trust you much if she makes you take all those pictures.

She has high standards, I said.

He drained the last of his beer and started on the second bottle. He said, My son wants to study in America when he's big.

Good, I said. Will he play basketball?

The man frowned. Of course not. That's just for fun. He's not tall enough to compete with Americans.

Oh, I said.

He wants to study computers.

That's great!

Your San Francisco is the place for that.

Sure, Silicon Valley. Google. Facebook. Steve Jobs.

Abruptly he stood, as though he'd had enough of my inane chatter. All right, then, he said. Are we done here?

My phone chimed and I checked the screen. Bags look good! Don't mind Ah Seng. He talks too much, but he's harmless.

This man, this Ah Seng, handed me an invoice, which I skimmed before signing my name. Once I'd paid for the bags from Winnie's account, I shook his hand, and ran for the door.

Outside on the street, I replied to Winnie's message. Her response was instantaneous. Good work! Went ahead and deposited your first installment.

I traced my way back to the peach-colored shopping center and checked the time. Fifteen minutes until my driver was due. I stepped into the building to escape the smog-filled air and found myself riding the escalator up to the Hermès boutique.

The same associate who'd helped me earlier was half-heartedly running a feather duster across the shelves. You're back, she said in a bored voice.

The amethyst Kelly was right where I'd left it. I slid my hand through its handle and turned to my reflection in the mirror on the wall. The bag dangled from my wrist like a graceful appendage; it transformed my basic cardigan and jeans into minimalist masterpieces; it made my heart race, like really good drugs.

It suits you, the girl said in her trademark deadpan.

You think so?

Our workmanship is one of a kind.

Two of a kind, really. You and Hermès.

She didn't crack a smile.

Eight thousand yuan is too much. I'll give you five.

The girl sprang to life. Five? No way I can do five.

I put the bag back on the shelf. I felt invincible. Forget it, I said. I have to meet my driver anyway.

Six-thousand-five, said the girl.

Six.

Done.

Every cell in my body thrummed in triumph. I paid the girl with my phone, and she swaddled my handbag as carefully as if it were a newborn and sent me on my way.

BY THE TIME I GOT back to my aunt and uncle's flat it was midafternoon. The curtains had been drawn shut against the harsh sun. On the sofa my aunt and uncle sat shellshocked, my softly snoring son curled up like a puppy at their feet. He finally exhausted himself, they whispered, and they hadn't dared to move him.

I had to beg my aunt and uncle to let me take them out to dinner that night to thank them for all they'd done. I chose a fancy seafood restaurant in Central that all the food blogs raved about and ordered the most costly items on the menu—wild clams, abalone, flower crabs—confident I could foot the bill this time around.

When my aunt asked what kind of tea I wanted, I said, Let's get wine.

At the end of the meal, I discovered three missed calls from Oli, and then, right before I went to bed, a long email detailing how sorry he was.

> I overreacted, I behaved horrendously. I hope you can forgive me.

He signed off with our inside joke: Ava, je t'aime beaucoup.

In the early days of our courtship, Oli had loved to poke fun at my textbook French—my perfect conjugations and musty vocabulary coupled with my complete inability to grasp the nuances of colloquial speech. A pair of expressions I found particularly infuriating: *je t'aime* and *je t'aime beaucoup*. It struck me as a somewhat barbed joke (on the part of the French) that contrary to the phrases' literal translations, "je t'aime" meant "I love you," while "je t'aime beaucoup" meant "I quite like you in a purely platonic way." After an impassioned debate on whether French or Chinese was the more xenophobic language (which, we agreed, ended in a draw), Oli had leaned in and kissed the tip of my nose and said, Je t'aime beaucoup. It's been our secret password ever since.

This message, right here, I saw as clear validation of

my decision to go to Guangzhou. I was proud of my re-
sourcefulness. I'd stood up to Oli, he'd backed down, and
the seesaw of our love had once again swung into balance.

Home on Thursday at 11. I wrote back. Je t'aime beaucoup.

FOR THE REST OF THE vacation, my family and I spent lazy
afternoons with my grandmother by the koi pond in the
courtyard of her nursing home, watching Henri gleefully
toss hunks of stale bread at the fish. We had scrumptious
dim sum lunches followed by long strolls through cool
shopping malls. We visited the aviary in Hong Kong Park,
and afterward, whenever Henri spotted a city sparrow,
he'd point to the sky and squawk.

One particular morning my aunt and I snuck away to
Pacific Place to do some shopping. On my own, without
Henri to corral, I marveled at how I didn't have to strain to
reach the subway handles, at how the jeans I tried on fell
to right above my anklebone, no hemming required, at how
every pair of shoes that caught my eye accommodated my
wide yet bony feet. For once in my life, my body wasn't a
problem to be solved. How different a person would I be, I
wondered, if I'd grown up in a place like this? Like my aunt
and my mom. Like Winnie.

Everything about the trip was perfect, except for the
way my uncle repeated, each time Henri made one of his
animal sounds, Don't worry, we'll get him talking, isn't that
right, little one? Say mom, dad, yes, no, dog, cat.

I tried to remember that Uncle Mark was trying to help, that my dad said the same kinds of things, that I was lucky to have these relatives in my life, and weren't relatives legally obligated to be a little bit annoying at least some of the time?

Whenever I raced my uncle to pay for a meal with my newly thawed credit card, my thoughts alighted on that bizarre day in the apartment with Ah Seng. Already it felt like something that had happened to someone else, a long time ago.

You see, Detective, in my mind, this thing with Winnie was over. Each of us had gotten what we'd needed; no one had been harmed.

On the last day of our trip, my aunt, Henri, and I returned to the nursing home to say goodbye to my grandmother. She was sitting in her wheelchair by the window, and when I walked into the room with Henri, she got so excited she forgot her legs were prone to giving way without warning and tried to stand.

My aunt hurried over saying, Don't get up!

As on all the previous afternoons, my son grew bashful and clung to me.

Call your great-grandmother, I urged. Tai-ma. Tai-ma.

He buried his head in my neck and I smiled apologetically at my grandma.

This time, instead of laughing it off, my grandma clucked impatiently. She held out her arms and demanded to hold him.

I felt his small body tense but lowered him to her all the same.

It's Taima, Cookie, I said, my pulse fluttering. You had so much fun with her yesterday. She gave you bread to feed the fish.

What did my son remember from day to day? What could account for his mercurial moods?

My grandma reached out and lightly pinched Henri's earlobe. The day before she'd said he had his great-grandfather's fleshy earlobes, a sign of good luck.

Henri wrenched away from her and began to howl. I wondered if he sensed something different about his great-grandmother, a whiff of acerbity that us adults were too desensitized to notice.

I explained that he hadn't slept well the previous night, but my grandmother ignored me, crowing, What a crybaby.

Ma, my aunt warned, placing a hand on her shoulder.

Come here, Henri, my grandma said. And then to my aunt, Don't you think he's too big to be crying all the time?

I set him on the ground and tried to turn him to her, but he mashed his face against my leg. At least he quieted down.

How old are you? my grandma asked.

He peered up at her sulkily.

Who's this? She pointed at me. Who's that? She pointed at Aunt Lydia. Silly boy, why can't you talk?

Blood pounded in my ears. If I'd been anywhere else, I would have enveloped Henri in my arms and whisked him away.

Too many questions, Ma, Aunt Lydia said. He's overwhelmed.

Right then, the sweet, chatty nurse I'd gotten to know over the past few days knocked on the door and held out a bag of stale bread to Henri. I seized the opportunity to move us all outside to the koi pond.

I wheeled my grandma to a shady spot beneath a lush tree with bright red leaves interspersed among the green. My aunt and I sat on the stone bench beside her, while Henri prowled the pond, searching for his favorite fish, the largest, with silver and vermillion spots.

Not too close, don't fall in, I called out from time to time.

My grandma was prodding me about when I planned to go back to work and whether Oli was a supportive husband when I noticed my son crouched low to the ground, gnawing on a heel of old bread.

I flew at him. Henri, no! It's old! It's only for fishies. I snatched up the plastic bag, which naturally devastated him. I held out my palm and ordered him to spit into it, and then gave up and cradled his heaving form.

From somewhere behind us, my grandma said to my aunt, What is with that child? Something isn't quite right in his head.

Suddenly I missed Oli fiercely. He who didn't hesitate

to tell busybodies to save their child-rearing advice for after they'd studied pediatric development and earned medical degrees.

Don't listen to them, I whispered in my son's ear, even as I made up my mind to use some of Winnie's money to take him to a speech therapist in secret.

You wonder, Detective, why it had to be secret? Because Oli would have declared it totally unnecessary and a big waste of money. He knew I was a worrier, you see, who needed constant reassurance that I was raising my kid right.

As usual, Oli would be correct. A month and a half after our return to San Francisco, the city's premier speech therapist would take one look at me and peg me for the high-achieving, overanxious mother that I was.

Go home, the therapist said. (I'm paraphrasing here.) He's two. As long as you're reading to him, he'll catch up.

I never told Oli about that visit. Why give him more reason to gloat?

7

A strange thing happened when Henri and I landed at SFO. Right before we disembarked, I removed my amethyst Kelly from my backpack, slid my wallet and passport into it, and slung it over my shoulder for the first time. This way, if Customs stopped us, they'd assume the bag was old. Pushing a dazed, half-dozing Henri in his stroller down the Customs line, I noticed passengers of all ages, from teenagers in faded jeans to grandmothers in orthopedic shoes, glancing my way. The pattern was always the same: their bored, tired gazes would sweep the hall, landing on my Kelly, and their eyes would swell in admiration and envy. Surreptitiously they studied my weary face, lank hair, rumpled clothes. How, they wondered, had such an ordinary-looking woman come to possess such a spectacular bag? Upon realizing that I'd caught them watching me, they invariably broke into shy smiles. I felt like a minor celebrity—a fashionista with a burgeoning social media following, a chef who'd made it through a couple rounds of a televised cooking contest. These strangers wanted to be me, or, at least, to be my friend.

So this was why people spent money on gigantic diamond rings, flashy sports cars; this was the allure of ostentatious-ness. To think I'd spent my entire adult life—perhaps my whole life—trying to disappear in dark, understated cloth-ing, sensible low-block heels. I'd had the same boring but flattering shoulder-length lob since junior year of college. I'd never once worn a shade of eye shadow that could not have been described as taupe.

Aside from this fake designer handbag hanging from my shoulder, had I ever chosen something simply because it made me happy? Henri's baby sneaker-socks with real shoelaces and rubber soles had made me happy. Oli's mother-of-pearl cuff links that I'd spotted in the window of a little shop in Aix-en-Provence had made me happy. But nothing I'd purchased for myself had ever elicited joy, not even my wedding dress, which I'd chosen for its reasonable price tag and, more importantly, its appropriateness. A silk cady column with a not-too-low V-neck and cap sleeves, it was a dress that made me look slender and flattered my skin tone and that could not, under any circumstances, be considered *in poor taste.*

In a way, wasn't this desire to disappear at the root of why I'd gone to law school despite having no interest in the law? Because it was easier and less risky to vanish into the image that my parents—and the world—had of the good Chinese American daughter? I bent over the stroller to make sure Henri's eyelids remained at half-mast. A long-ago image surfaced of freshman-year Winnie in a pink

T-shirt with the words CUTY PIE plastered across the front
in multicolored rhinestones. At the time, my friends and I
mocked her behind her back, but now I wondered how she
would have reacted if I'd done it to her face.

Her retort rose in my ears. What would you suggest
I wear? One of three identical black sweaters every day?
Don't you ever get bored? What do you want to wear? Do
you have any idea, Ava, what it is you actually want?

In the Lyft back home, I imagined potential additions to
my wardrobe: crimson patent leather heels, a leopard-print
swing coat, something, anything trimmed in fur. What if?
I thought. What if? What if? This must seem so frivolous
to you, Detective, but trust me when I say this new line
of questioning was nothing short of revolutionary. Never
before had I so casually dismissed the things I believed I
should want and should do and should be.

I was still lost in daydreams when a message from Winnie lit up my phone. Bags arrived. They are perfect! Best workmanship yet. Call when you've settled to discuss next steps.

I didn't have time to reply because the car had arrived
at the house, and the sight of Oli's BMW in the driveway
wiped away all other thoughts.

The driver hauled our suitcase from the trunk, and I
lifted out the car seat holding my still-sleeping son.

Papa's home, I whispered.

Oli was in the living room, typing furiously on his laptop.

When I set down the car seat, Henri opened one eye,
frowned, and tugged on his ear, but the sight of his father

halted his tears. Oli took him in his arms and covered him with kisses. He stroked his hair and said, Tu me manques. (You are missed by me—another of those infuriating French-isms.)

Over Henri's tousled head, Oli's gaze latched on to mine.

Hi, he said.

Hello.

Henri whined and rubbed his eyes, and Oli said he'd put him down for a nap.

I rolled the suitcase into the bedroom, listening to Oli tell Henri how much he loved him. The bed was exactly as I'd left it—the duvet hastily pulled up, my pillow still bearing the indentation of my skull. Oli hadn't slept here the entire time we'd been away. I opened a window to clear the must.

Eventually I noticed Oli in the doorway, watching me unpack.

Hi, I said.

Hello. The corners of his mouth twitched.

I felt strangely shy.

He said, I'm going to give up the apartment. We'll move down as a family—when you're ready.

It was everything I wanted, and yet, when I took in the purple crescents beneath his eyes and the stubble on his chin I said, No, don't. I know how hard you work.

His eyebrows jumped.

I was being selfish. Keep the apartment for now. I can manage with Maria.

In a timid voice he asked, Are you sure?

I'm sure.

That afternoon, for the first time in weeks, we made love. And for the first time in longer than that, my insides roiled like the sea. When I stunned him by climbing on top and straddling him—something I hadn't done since the very beginning—he released a guttural moan, a sound so reflexive, so intimate, it filled me with tenderness, pure and honey-sweet.

Afterward we lay on the twisted sheets, holding each other until Henri summoned us with a wail. We grabbed him from his room and ordered in saag paneer and chicken tikka masala. We ate with abandon until our waistbands grew tight. Oli surprised Henri with a shiny train set, and they spent an hour making those little wooden train cars go around the track. When Oli started to yawn, I told him to go to sleep; I'd stay up with our jet-lagged boy.

It was after midnight when I crawled into bed and fit my body around my husband's, basking in his heat. I awoke at dawn to find he'd already left to beat traffic.

I waited a few hours before calling to tell Winnie there'd be no next steps; our business relationship was done.

These bags are truly stellar, she said by way of greeting. What I need you to do next is open a business credit card, make up a name, something mundane.

I interrupted. There is no next time. I'm not getting involved in all that.

What are you talking about? You're already involved.

That was different. Those were extenuating circum-stances.

Her incredulousness seemed sincere. Come on, Ava, you did all the heavy lifting. This is the fun part, the reward for your hard work. Here's your chance to make the easy money.

All I had to do, she said, was take my new credit card to the Chanel boutique on Geary and purchase a Gabrielle. And then, a couple days later, I'd return the twin superfake in its place.

It certainly didn't sound like fun. Even I knew that boutiques posed a bigger challenge than department stores, their salespeople more exacting, their return policies less generous.

When I pointed this out, Winnie said, Ava, your bags are that good. We have to go for it. The boutiques have the widest breadth of styles. That's where the money is.

It's hard to explain the feeling her words unleashed inside of me, the tingling in the bowl of my belly, the bright-ness behind my eyes. I imagined striding into that store, swinging my Kelly bag, slapping down my credit card. What was it like, I wondered, to be so brash, so bold? And what if I could slip on that persona, just for a moment, as easily as I could a mink stole?

Winnie was still talking. In a couple months, we'll send you to Dongguan to meet Boss Mak and our other part-ners, introduce you more officially.

I snapped out of the fantasy—because that's all it was: make-believe, fiction, farce.

Hold on, I said. Definitely not. For even if I'd wanted to go, which I did not, how would I explain it to Oli? We'd only recently made up.

Oh, so he finally apologized?

What do you mean? I asked. I'd never mentioned the frozen bank cards.

Coolly she said, I ran into Oli while you were gone. Didn't he tell you?

Her studied nonchalance had me on guard. Where? Palo Alto? What were you doing down there?

In the city. At that seafood place in Union Square. Farelly? Farolo? Some funny name like this.

Farallon. I knew the restaurant, the kind of hushed, over-priced joint that appealed to finance guys—and their lovers.

That's the one.

Who was he with? How did he look? What did he say?

Calm down, Ava. He was with colleagues. They were about to leave, and he looked so glum that I convinced him to stay and have another round.

Of course, I bristled. What must Oli's colleagues have thought when he'd begged off to have a drink with an at-tractive woman? Why hadn't Oli mentioned this?

But Winnie insisted he'd spoken only of me and Henri.

What did you say to him? I asked.

Exactly what I thought. That he'd gone too far. That he was behaving no differently from those old raging patri-archs in China who demand that their wives and children submit to their every whim. That he was better than this.

In replaying this scene, Detective, I see that she couldn't have run into him by accident. She must have had her private investigator tail him to the restaurant and spy on his table, so she could appear at an opportune time. I wonder how she got Oli not only to open up but also to admit that he was in the wrong. She certainly went to a whole load of trouble to intervene in our little marital spat. But this way I owed her one, this way I was in her debt.

THIS IS HOW, ON A fine, cloudless afternoon, I found myself driving over thirty miles to the Stanford Shopping Center, with Winnie riding shotgun and a large Chanel shopping bag in the back seat.

Believe me when I say I tried multiple times to back out. In fact, the whole plan was so repulsive, I'd been sick to my stomach for the past forty-eight hours, prompting Maria to ask if I was pregnant, or had the flu. But each time I told Winnie I couldn't go through with the return, she harnessed her masterful skills of persuasion to prove me wrong.

Ava, she said, what makes a fake bag fake if it's indistinguishable from the real thing? What gives the real bag its inherent value?

I had to admit she had a point: the real and knock-off Gabrielles were exact duplicates, from the brushed antique-gold logos to the gilded authenticity cards in their crisp letterpress envelopes. Before Winnie had posted the real one online for five percent below list price (and it had been snapped up within the hour), I'd stuck my nose into each bag and inhaled its identical musky scent—a reminder that this tanned, dyed skin had once been part of a living, breathing whole.

When I continued to insist that it wasn't in my nature to deceive, she said, Just try it this once. Oli will never know. No one will. Come on, Ava, admit it, isn't it fun to bend the rules a little?

Here's the thing, Detective. All through my teenage years, I'd never once snuck out of the house, or missed curfew, or owned a fake ID. Why? Fear, I guess. Guilt. In those days, closing my eyes and picturing my mom's dismay was enough to make me abandon whatever minor act of rebellion had crossed my mind. I told myself I'd have fun once I went to college, or once I lived on my own, or once I was financially independent and answered to no one. But eventually resignation set in, and habit, too. And so here I was, thirty-seven years old and feeling cheated out of the chance to collect the wild, silly stories one told about one's youth.

You know, my mom died four months before she planned to retire. She'd already booked her and my dad's first postretirement vacation: two weeks in Tuscany, hiking, cooking, sipping wine under the sun. Again, I don't want to make excuses, but I think it's fair to note that when Winnie reentered my life, I was racked with regret—for all the experiences I'd postponed and then lost, for all the moments my mom would never have, and that she and I would never share. Surely it's clear that any master manipulator would have nailed me for an easy mark.

As I cruised past the last San Francisco exit on 280, fingers clenching the steering wheel, I made a final attempt.

Please, Winnie, don't make me go through with this. I didn't have to glance at her to know her patience was wearing thin.

But she, too, had one final card. I'd mentioned that I'd gotten Henri an appointment with the coveted speech therapist, and now she said, casually, How much per session?

Three fifty.

And you can't tell Oli?

Never.

And let's say she wants to see Henri once a week for six months, maybe a year. How do you plan to pay for it?

I stared straight ahead. She placed a warm palm on the back of my neck.

Stop worrying, she said. It'll be over in five minutes.

I veered off the freeway while she repeated bits of the same pep talk she'd first given when we left the city.

Not too many excuses, that's what sounds fishy. Be confident. Polite. Firm.

In the mall parking lot, I pulled into a spot, and a shiny white Tesla glided in next to me. A group of Chinese girls — college students from Stanford, or possibly, Santa Clara — tumbled out of the car like lithe, nimble clowns.

Winnie observed that these days there were so many

Mainland Chinese in American universities, not like during our time, when there were only a few.

I don't remember you hanging out with other Mainlanders, I said.

Back then you had to be very connected and powerful to send your child abroad. Those kids wouldn't have been friends with me. Besides, why would I come all this way to spend time with other Chinese?

She told me how thrilled she was to find out I was her roommate — a real American!

I felt suddenly moved that she'd thought of me that way. I recalled how annoyed I used to get by her ceaseless questions about the most seemingly random topics: Would your parents be mad if you dated a white? What about a Black? Does your mom make Chinese or American food? Did your parents beat you when you were small? Not beat — hit, yes, spank.

Winnie opened the passenger door, and when she saw me waver, she sat back and said, Think of it this way. These salespeople spend their time handling luxuries they can't afford themselves, pandering to the superrich and superentitled.

So?

So it doesn't take much to get someone like that on your side, to make them want to help you.

I released my seat belt.

Remember, don't talk so much.

I stepped out of the car. I'd tried to emulate Winnie by donning a loose silk shirt tucked into black cigarette pants.

She scanned me from head to toe, zeroing in on my black leather shoulder bag—a French contemporary brand, Sandro or maybe A.P.C.—that had been a gift from Oli's mom.

She hooked a finger at me. Give me that. You carry mine.

I dutifully handed over my bag. The one she gave me in exchange, an Hermès Evelyne, was, quite frankly, nothing special, even somewhat unattractive: a flat gray rectangle of soft pebbled leather, with a utilitarian cross-body strap and a large H perforated into the side that was meant to be hidden, but which most people wore facing outward.

My doubts must have registered on my face because Winnie assured me that the Evelyne was a key part of the costume.

It shows you're rich but not flashy.

I slung the bag over my shoulder, H side out, and followed behind her.

She stopped dead. Ava, she said, rolling her palms skyward, the Gabrielle.

I scurried back to the car for the shopping bag, and we set off once again.

In the years since we'd been students, a thorough renovation had transformed the already swanky Stanford Shopping Center into an oasis of excessive luxury. Graceful walkways lined by floral planters in full bloom marked the path to each jeweled, perfumed boutique. Coiffed patrons lounged on gilded chairs scattered about the manicured courtyards. The entire sprawling burnished compound formed a facsimile of a picturesque square in a second-tier European city, sans the hordes of sweating tourists, the pollution, the charm. This overwhelming abundance of artificial beauty contributed, once again, to the feeling that I'd entered a fantasy realm, where absolutely nothing, including the crime I was about to commit, was real.

When the Chanel boutique came into view, Winnie stationed herself at a wrought-iron table paces from the entrance.

What are you waiting for? she asked.

I wiped my damp palms on the seat of my pants and made for the store.

A security guard in a black suit held open the heavy glass door with a murmured, Good afternoon, madam.

A wave of deliciously cold air, infused with the heady, expensive scent of roses, swept me inside. The boutique was all shiny surfaces, golden light. A pair of saleswomen in pencil skirts and crisp white shirts stood like sentries behind glass counters on opposite sides of the room. One was likely Mainland Chinese, to cater to all the Mandarin-speaking big spenders; the other was white and middle-aged. Before the conscious part of my brain had made a decision, my body instinctively veered toward the white woman.

Her eyes glinted behind oversized tortoiseshell glasses. How can I help you today?

Sweat sprang from my armpits. I clamped my elbows to my sides to hide the burgeoning stains and said, Just a return. I set my shopping bag on the counter.

Let's have a look, shall we?

Why hadn't Winnie warned me against wearing silk? Moving only my forearms, I gingerly pulled out the dust bag containing the replica Gabrielle.

In the mirror I watched the Chinese woman stifle a yawn and stroll out of hearing distance, and the muscles deep within my abdomen unclenched.

Well, this is a surprise, the associate said.

My muscles tightened once more.

Beige and black is our most popular color combination. The wait list's a mile long. You're sure you don't want it?

It's not really my style, I said. And then hastily added, I mean, I thought it was when I bought it, but I changed my mind when I got home.

Shut up, I told myself. I didn't know what to do with my hands. I reached in Winnie's bag for my phone and checked the time.

The associate regarded Winnie's Evelyne. I understand. You're more of a minimalist.

Exactly, I said. What had Winnie said about her bag? I repeated, I prefer things that are understated, less flashy.

The associate's eyes lit up. I know what you mean. She lowered her voice. To be honest, even I sometimes find our things a little fussy. She pressed an index finger to her lips and giggled.

I grazed her forearm with my fingertips and giggled along.

Giving the Gabrielle one last cursory glance, she scanned my receipt.

Do you need my credit card?

No, you're all set. Four thousand six hundred and sixty-five back onto your Visa. She printed out a new receipt, attached it to the old one with a glossy black paper clip, and then folded both into a cream envelope.

I thanked her and then willed myself to walk slowly out of the store, one step at a time, like a bridesmaid proceeding down the aisle.

Have a good day, the security guard intoned, and I couldn't help breaking into a grin.

When I emerged, Winnie was still seated at the same table, looking at her phone. Like a fool, I waved madly. Her face twisted into a grimace. I dropped my hand.

Miss! a voice called from behind me. Miss! Hang on!

My stomach lurched, as though spurring me to take off running down the exquisitely landscaped path. What choice did I have but to turn around?

The associate held out my cell phone. You left this on the counter.

Oh, I said, retrieving the phone. Thank you so much.

Not at all. Come back and see us again. We'll find something that's more your style.

Winnie and I headed for the parking lot. I waited until we'd rounded the corner to collapse against a pillar, euphoric with relief. Never again, I said. I'm not cut out for this. My nerves can't handle it.

She shook her head. You're absolutely right for this. You have an honest face, and you're Asian American. No one would ever suspect a thing.

8

After Chanel, I resolved to be done with Winnie once and for all. I made it clear that I could not work for her. I screened her calls, claimed to be too busy to meet up when she came to town. And there was plenty of truth to my excuses. We were entering that fraught and stressful period known as preschool interview month, and I had to keep my calendar open in the event that one of the eight schools we'd applied to summoned us in for a visit.

I spent the rest of February refreshing my email and scanning the mommy message boards, torturing myself by reading every celebratory thread. In March the rejections streamed in, one after another. We regret to inform you. Record number of applications. Many more qualified students. We are sorry, truly wish, sincerely hope.

Oli coped by making barbed jokes of the they-don't-deserve-our-son variety. Me? I cursed myself for telling everyone in our circle that we'd applied this year and prayed they wouldn't bring it up. I wondered if I could spin a credible tale about deciding against sending Henri so early; after all, he was not yet two and a half.

But then, one afternoon, seven rejections later, our last hope, Divisadero Prep, wrote to tell us we'd been moved on to the next and final round. The playdate-slash-interview was scheduled for the following Tuesday at 9 a.m., and I set out to do everything in my power to ensure it would go smoothly.

On the morning itself, Maria and Henri and I were fifteen minutes early. As the message board moms advised, arrive too early and your toddler might get bored; arrive too late and he won't have time to adjust and could grow cranky and confused. I parked on the shady side of the street and rolled down the windows to let in the breeze.

In the back seat, Maria and Henri played round after round of patty-cake. Each time she chanted, Roll it up, pat it, and mark it with an H—drawing the letter across his belly with her finger—he bounced up and down like a bobblehead doll. Everything had lined up in our favor. Henri was in a great mood. He'd slept well the night before, waking briefly only once. Maria had made his favorite breakfast of blueberry-chocolate-chip pancakes, which he'd downed with gusto. I'd dressed him in the cutest little peach Lacoste polo shirt that brought out the pink in his cheeks. (Do your best to ensure that your toddler is neither hungry, nor thirsty, nor exhausted, nor dirty, the moms counseled.)

From time to time Maria's eyes flickered down to her watch, a tic that revealed her to be as anxious as I was.

With ten minutes to go, she lifted Henri in the air, sniffed his butt, and patted it twice. Smells like roses, she said. I think he's all set. She cupped Henri's face in both hands. Have fun at school, mi amor.

Not for the first time I wished I could send Maria into the classroom with him. When the school had specified that each prospective student arrive with one caregiver, they'd obviously meant a parent, but what if I gave a valid excuse? Like, I had to leave town because of a death in the family? Or I was busy getting chemo? Yes, that's how much of a wreck I was.

Let's go, Cookie, I sang inanely. Maria, we'll be back in an hour. I opened the passenger door and hoisted Henri out of the car, and he twisted around and held out his hand to his nanny.

Her smile froze. I'll be right here, mi amor, she said, waving.

He opened and closed his palm insistently, a tiny despot demanding to be paid.

It's just you and me, Cooks, I said, steering him to face me. It'll be fun. You'll get to play with your new classmates.

I tried to lead him away but he squirmed out of my grasp and clung to the hem of Maria's T-shirt. She gently pried him loose. Go with Mama.

He scowled and tugged on his ear.

Okay, okay, I said. What if Maria walks us to the gate and we say goodbye there?

She was already getting out of the car. She hefted Henri

into her arms, and the whimpering stopped. This was precisely the scenario we'd hoped to avoid, for surely there would be a teacher standing at the gate to greet us, and her first impression could not be of a boy screaming for his nanny.

We walked slowly, Maria and I searching for a way to avert the impending disaster.

Remember what I told you? she said to Henri. You're a big boy now and big boys go to school.

He gnawed placidly on a hank of her hair.

There'll be lots of new toys. And the teacher will teach you games and songs and give you yummy snacks.

By now we were half a block away from the school, and I said, How about Mama carry you now?

Maria freed her hair from his grasp. Yes, go to Mama.

She and I had landed on the same plan; she would slow down behind us, and I would hurry him inside and distract him, hopefully before he noticed she was gone. But when I extended my arms to him, he burrowed his face into Maria's bosom.

Mi amor, she whispered, it's only for a little while. Maria will be right outside waiting. Had the stakes not been so high, she would never have said that in front of me—she, who always took care not to spark parental jealousy.

Honestly, though, I was too stressed for her words to sting. (Try to exude tranquility, the moms cautioned. If you're tense, your toddler will notice and tense up too.)

We were no more than ten paces from the school gate. I watched a tall white woman with a platinum-blond ponytail stride toward it with a matching oversized blond child, who enthusiastically high-fived the teacher standing guard.

Frances Wright, the woman said, holding out her hand. Tell her your name, honey, she prompted her son.

Spencer Alexander Wright, said the boy, adorably adding, Very pleased to meet you.

The teacher's face brightened. The pleasure is mine, she said, checking them off on her clipboard and letting them through. She scribbled a note by the boy's name, no doubt urging the admissions committee to accept this charming, articulate child. Looking up, she spotted the three of us picking our way toward her and waved. I waved back. Maria kept right on whispering in Henri's ear. Whatever she told him worked, because when she set him down, he reached for my hand.

Good luck, have fun, Maria said, and then her footsteps receded down the sidewalk.

Ready, Cooks? I asked.

He gazed up at me and chortled like I'd told the best joke.

You must be Ava, the teacher said. And you must be Henri. She bent over so she was eye level with him, and my heart soared when he let her shake his hand.

We were taken to a classroom with the other prospective students—five in all, plus four moms and one dad.

The teacher supervising the playdate introduced herself as Ms. Jenny and instructed us parents to take a seat on the miniature chairs lined up against the far wall.

Ms. Jenny had Shirley Temple curls and large shiny teeth like a horse. Sit back and relax, she said, which prompted nervous laughter, plus a hoot from the dad. This time is for the kids to explore the classroom and have fun. That's it! There's nothing else on the agenda.

The dad gave a little snort. He had reddish scruff on his chin, a silver hoop in one ear, and an overly friendly demeanor. I resolutely ignored him, already annoyed. The platinum-haired woman retrieved a notebook from her Evelyne bag (rouge tomate, Clemence leather) and scrawled something in it. Was she writing down what Ms. Jenny said? Was she taking notes on her child? On our children? Who knew?

The teacher gave the kids a tour of the classroom, pointing out the shelf of board books, the table stacked with coloring sheets and crayons, the bin filled with dolls and stuffed animals and trucks and planes, the basin of home-made playdough, the Lego corner. The kids scattered about the room. A half Asian, half white girl with two tiny pigtails sticking straight out of her head knelt by the bookshelf and chose a book, and I oozed envy.

The dad spoke out of the corner of his mouth. Cecily's favorite thing to do is read.

Aha, an Asian wife, who must have worked in tech or finance and made a boatload of money if this man, her husband, was the primary caregiver. The dad waved at his little reader, displaying a tattoo on the inside of his wrist that read [sic].

Henri and Spencer Alexander Wright went straight for the construction toys, and my fingers gripped the seat of my chair. The bigger boy got there first and plucked out the shiny yellow bulldozer, which Henri wanted too. He stood there, looking deflated and bewildered, and I held my breath and prayed. And then, instead of pressing his case, Henri simply dug through the bin and found another shabbier, smaller bulldozer. I wanted to leap up and cheer. I looked over at the teacher to see if she'd noticed my son's magnanimity, but she was watching another toddler draw long orange streaks across a page.

That one's mine, I said to the dad, who replied generously, What a good sport.

For the next twenty minutes or so, we parents murmured and chuckled and gawked as though playtime were a most engrossing piece of theater. When Ms. Jenny announced that it was time for the children to move on to another activity of their choice, I tried to signal to Henri with a subtle flick of my chin. Books. Go to the books.

He took his time, roaming the room, watching the other kids.

So watchful, I observed softly. Such a thinker.

Little Cecily was apparently completely absorbed in *The Very Hungry Caterpillar* because she kept turning pages, paying the teacher no mind. Ms. Jenny approached and told her it was time to try something else, and she scrunched up her face and flung the book on the floor with a prolonged screech.

Henri looked over with concern, but the teacher was too occupied to notice his deep well of empathy.

It's okay, Cece, the dad called out. I'm sorry, Ms. Jenny, she loves that book so much. He rose from his chair, but the teacher stayed him with a shake of her head.

In a calm voice she said, Cecily, it's time for another activity.

The little girl grabbed the book and chucked it straight at Ms. Jenny's sternum.

Ouch, said the teacher.

The girl giggled, probably more from surprise than from malice.

Cece, the dad yelled, say you're sorry.

The girl ran over to her dad, who ordered her once again to apologize.

She looked over her shoulder and sang, almost coquettishly, Soooorry.

She's very sorry, he said. He pushed her toward Ms. Jenny. Say it like you mean it.

Cecily slinked over to the teacher. She looked up at her through long lashes and gave her the most alluring grin. I'm sorry, Ms. Jenny.

The teacher patted her grimly on the head.

The rest of us parents clucked, charmed and horrified by this beguiling child and, above all, relieved our own kid hadn't been the one to act out.

Behind me, one mom said to another, The most advanced are always the most willful.

The platinum-haired woman called out, Good job, Spence!, when her son hammered a rubber nail into a plank, which prompted a pointed look from Ms. Jenny.

Henri wandered past the bookshelf and landed, finally, at the table with the playdough basin. Good choice. Playdough was safe. It couldn't be jabbed or hurled or otherwise used as a weapon. A little later, Cecily joined Henri at the table, a wonderful chance for him to demonstrate how well he played with others. For a few enchanting moments, the two of them stood side by side, companionably molding lumps of dough.

Look, Cecily said, taking her lump and pancaking it on the table, which Henri found hilarious. Mimicking her, he, too, pounded his lump flat. Apparently, he now felt like he owed her something in return because he peeled his pancake off the table and gleefully nibbled its edge.

The girl's eyes widened and then she threw back her head and laughed. I inhaled long and slow. The dough was just flour and water (and dirt from the hands of innumerable preschoolers). It would be fine. Ms. Jenny wouldn't even notice.

Henri must have decided the playdough tasted pretty good, though, because he took another nibble. Now this was too much for Cecily, who flagged down the teacher like she was hailing a taxi and shouted, Baby eat playdough!

The dad slapped his knee. She's so bossy. My wife says she has the personality of a CEO, and she would know.

I wanted to throttle him and, to be honest, the little girl, too, but I couldn't take my eyes off my son, who balled up his pancake and licked it like a lollypop.

He never does that, I called out. Cookie, don't be silly, stop it.

Ms. Jenny glanced at his name tag. Henri, playdough isn't for eating.

Henri's big brown eyes gazed up at her. He slowly unfurled his tongue. I sank into my tiny chair.

No, she said, taking the playdough from his hand.

He craned to look at me, his eyes filling with tears.

I shook my head and mouthed, You're fine. Don't cry. I love you.

He pulled on his earlobe and released a chilling scream.

The moms behind me gasped. Cecily made a big show of stuffing her fingers in her ears. I couldn't stop myself from shooting her a dirty look as I hurried to my all-out-wailing child.

(Don't be afraid to take your toddler outside for air, said the moms. You're the parent!)

I'll take him outside for a bit, I said, surprised when Ms. Jenny simply nodded.

What did this mean? That she'd already made up her mind about him? That no further observation was necessary?

I carried Henri up and down the hallway, pushing his

face into my sleeve to muffle his sobs. Still, a teacher in another classroom stuck out her head and told us to quiet down. Out in the front yard, I searched hopefully for Maria, but she was back at the car.

Look, Henri, I said, pointing at a sparrow on a branch, but he appeared to only take interest in the birds of Hong Kong.

Patty-cake, patty-cake, I said, holding up my hand for him to slap.

He squeezed his eyes shut and cried harder.

Did Ms. Jenny make you feel bad? She didn't mean to, I don't think. Or was it Cecily? You don't have to play with her when you go back in there.

Henri was inconsolable.

Please, Cookie, we have to go back. Just for a few minutes.

He mournfully shook his head.

Ten minutes, I promise.

And then, a gift from the heavens: a bulldozer was ambling along this very block.

Look, Cooks, I cried, and this time, he perked up and waved and waved, and the driver, a veritable angel, tipped his hard hat in response. I wiped my son's snot, blotted the drool from his shirt collar as best I could, and hustled him inside. But by then we'd missed cleanup and sharing circle and the playdate was over.

Can we come back another day? I asked Ms. Jenny as the other parents filed out with their sweet, saintly children.

I'm afraid not, the teacher said.

Please, I said. He's very shy. He's an only child. He'll get used to being around other kids.

This is our last session. Letters go out next week.

Could he sit in on a real class? Or meet a few more teachers? I could hear the frenzy creep into my voice. He's really lovely once you get to know him.

I'm sure that's true, Ms. Jenny said kindly, which made me feel worse. He's going to find the right school, whether it's here or someplace else.

It has to be here, I said. We love this school. It's our only choice.

The teacher gave me a smile that stopped short of her eyes. It will all work out. You'll see.

A loud crash hijacked our attention. Henri had swept every last book off the bottom shelf and cackled at his accomplishment.

Oh, Cooks, what did you do? I fell to my knees and started shoving books back onto the shelf.

Leave it, said Ms. Jenny.

Absolutely not, I said.

Her tone was sharp. No, really, leave it. She sighed. You're shelving them wrong. I'll just have to do it all over again.

I set down *The Cat in the Hat*, got to my feet, and took my son's hand. Together he and I walked to the car, where Maria sprang up, asking, How was it? How'd he do? Did you have fun, mi amor?

I shook my head, and she pressed her lips together and said no more.

Oli, of course, would not be so easily silenced.

He called as I was pulling out of the parking spot, and I put him on speakerphone.

What do you mean? Disastrous how?

I recounted the whole morning.

He's a baby. They of all people should know how babies act.

It's over, I said.

Not necessarily. Did you explain that this was an anomaly? Did you ask to bring him back again?

Yes, I replied to every one of his questions, until, at last he said, We can still fix this. I'm sure of it.

If you're so sure, you fix it. I glanced into the rearview mirror, and Maria politely avoided my gaze.

Hang on, he said.

I heard him say something brusque and important-sounding to an unknown colleague.

I have to go, he said. Call your friend Winnie. Didn't she teach kindergarten?

I was taken aback that he'd remembered. What's she supposed to do about it?

With exaggerated patience he said, Well, I don't know, Ava, that's why you have to call her and ask.

WINNIE ANSWERED THE PHONE RIGHT away.

I'm sorry it's taken me so long to call you back, I said.

It's totally fine, she said. I know you've been busy.

My eyes stung. It seemed like it had been weeks, maybe months, since anyone had been kind to me. I said, It's been awful over here.

I told her about the playdate, and after I explained the teacher's unfairness, Winnie said, To tell you the truth, I don't know why people think that school's so good. They don't seem like anything special to me.

Already I felt better.

She said, Tell you what, I'll call my friend Florence Lin at Ming Liang Academy in the Richmond.

I pointed out that it was too late. Every decent school's application period had closed in January. Notifications would go out any day now.

Winnie gave me that bark of a laugh. Florence is a friend. We taught together in Culver City. She'll accept Henri with my recommendation.

Was she serious? Could it be this easy? We hadn't looked into Chinese immersion schools, since Oli was already teaching Henri French, but Ming Liang had a good reputation.

Henri will love it there, she said.

You really think this'll work? Winnie had never mentioned this friend of hers before, and I wondered what she'd done for Florence to be owed this favor.

Of course. And if you don't want to take any chances, make a small donation. A couple grand will do.

I hesitated.

What's wrong? Even three, four grand is enough. Just

a small percentage of what you're already spending on school fees.

It wasn't the money I was worried about; it was my husband. I could already hear his rant: *We're not bribing our son's way into preschool, Ava. Don't be absurd.*

I quickly calculated how much I had left in my WeChat account and realized that just as Oli didn't need to know about Henri's upcoming visit to the pricey speech therapist, he wouldn't need to know about this.

I told Winnie I'd be happy to make a donation, and she said, Great, I'll call Florence right now.

Thank you, I said. I mean it.

She brushed it off. What are friends for?

By the week's end, an official acceptance letter from Ming Liang Academy had arrived in the mail. My husband got his *I told you so* and I was further ensnared in Winnie's web, biding time until whenever she decided to collect.

9

Winnie gave me a couple weeks to celebrate Henri's pre-school acceptance, and then she texted to inform me she was back in town. Meet me at Bloomingdale's, Westfield Mall, 2pm. She provided no additional details.

You have the security footage, Detective; you saw how quickly she put me back to work, sending me on assignments at least once a week. Her goal was to make these store returns habitual, to help me relax. She told me I needed to stop worrying, that the more I could sink into the role, the less likely I was to actually get caught.

And I must admit, the lawyer in me appreciated the pure elegance of her scheme. Not even the most discerning shopper would doubt the authenticity of a bag purchased from a reputable retailer. The power of suggestion was too seductive, the confirmation bias effect too potent.

Soon, Winnie declared me ready to go off on my own. As your videos show, each week I would test out a different persona depending on the store. Here I am in Barneys (RIP), as the impatient, high-powered career woman on her lunch break; that's me, too, at Saks, the indecisive middle manager who only recently started buying luxury; at Gucci, the flighty trophy wife; at Louis Vuitton, the spoiled heiress; and here at Nordstrom, my favorite of them all, I am the down-to-earth stay-at-home mom, which is to say, more or less myself.

Why did I love Nordstrom? Let me count the ways. They had the most forgiving return policy on the planet. Their sales staff were friendly and efficient, and, most importantly, refrained from asking questions. Their downtown location was busy enough that I never felt like I was being watched, which, in turn, let me do the watching.

Lurking around the cash wrap, I'd seen customers return blatantly used clothing, shoes, even underwear, with no tags, no receipts, nothing except their dubious claims. These people made me feel comparatively virtuous. After all, the store would have no difficulty selling my replica Longchamp Le Pliage (size L, in lemon yellow). Nordstrom wasn't losing a cent off me.

One time, I watched a middle-aged white woman pull a beat-up pair of hiking boots out of a paper grocery bag. The shoes were so battered she probably saw no point in fudging the truth and readily offered that they'd been purchased a year earlier. Apparently, she'd recently gained twenty pounds (due to new medication), which had caused her feet to spread, and now the blasted things gave her blisters.

The sales associate's smile never dimmed as he gingerly

turned over one boot and said, Oh, wow, we haven't carried this brand in a while.

The woman shrugged. Okay, well, what can you do for me?

Her sense of entitlement floored me. Would it have killed her to look sorry?

The associate said, How about you pick out another pair of hiking boots and we do a straight swap? He added, If you don't like what we have in store, we can order a pair online and have them delivered to your home?

Instead of falling over herself in gratitude, the woman said, I don't really need hiking boots. What I need is a sturdy pair of sandals. Can I get some of those?

The associate's forehead creased. I edged closer and pretended to study a pair of rubber flip-flops dangling from a rack. Was history about to be made? Had the Nordstrom return policy finally met its match?

The associate called over a manager, and they conferred for a few minutes before he announced, Good news! We can make that work!

Later, I'd recount the story to Winnie, who'd offer that she'd once seen someone return a faded plaid work shirt so old a hole had formed in one armpit seam.

Did he even give a reason?

Yes, the reason was the hole.

Winnie told me that ridiculously generous return policies had been one of the things that amazed her about America. Right up there with portion size, four-way stops, and water wastage. One hundred percent customer satisfaction, she said. That's the American way.

I guess what I'm saying, Detective, is that Winnie convinced me that ours was a benign and victimless crime. For didn't everyone in the equation go home happy? The online customer got to purchase a coveted designer handbag for a fair price from our eBay shop, the sales associate made a good commission from unwittingly selling a counterfeit, and even the customer to whom said counterfeit was sold very likely left satisfied. (And, if not, could easily make a return.) As long as this was the case, what did it matter that only one of those bags was the real thing?

Armed with this questionable pseudosubjectivist logic, Winnie pushed me to take on ever more consequential responsibilities. When I balked at inventory arriving at my door—what if Maria mistakenly opened a box?—Winnie told me to rent a unit in a nondescript South San Francisco office park. When I complained about being assigned too many returns, she had me hire and train more shoppers. Before I knew it, I'd turned into a one-woman HR department—and Winnie's right hand. As she well knew, my entire career as an unhappy lawyer had primed me for this job. For the first time in my working life, I was managing an entire process from start to finish, seeing the immediate, tangible results of my labor, and that, after years of paperwork for the sake of paperwork, was groundbreaking.

By this point, our annual revenue was clearing two million, fifteen percent of which Winnie sent to Boss Mak per the terms of their original agreement. She paid me a sizable salary, too—as much as I'd made at the firm (in half the hours), a portion of which I gladly spent on Maria's overtime.

No, I don't think Maria has any idea what we were doing. In fact, I'm sure of it. All I'd told her was that I was helping my friend Winnie, reviewing contracts, advising on tariffs and tax issues, you know, boring stuff. I assume you gathered as much from her deposition? Once or twice, she might have opened the trunk of my car to find it packed with handbags, but I said it was for a charity fundraiser. Yes, of course I still consider her family. Why, does your family know each and every detail of your life?

I didn't mean to snap. I guess I still regret the way she and I grew apart, and, more broadly, the way the constant lying took its toll on all my friendships. What Maria and I shared was real—we weren't close in that fake treacly way that rich neoliberals are with their household help. I truly valued our relationship. Over tea and lemon cookies during Henri's naptime, she'd vent about the men her sister kept trying to set her up with and her dad's conservative political views, and I confided in her, too. She was the first person to whom I admitted that I hated being a lawyer, months before I even told my husband.

I have only myself to blame for what happened. One afternoon in April, about three months into working for Winnie, I was driving back from South San Francisco and got stuck on the freeway—a horrific car crash involving an overturned big rig. Traffic was bumper-to-bumper. I literally didn't move for half an hour. Amid this gridlock, Oli texted to say he'd left work early and was on his way home. I knew there was a chance he'd beat me there and find Maria with Henri.

He, too, had no clue how much time I devoted to this work. I'd told him the same things I'd told Maria—that I was just keeping busy helping Winnie while I explored job options, and that yes, of course, she was paying me. I arranged for five thousand dollars to be deposited into the joint account each month. He didn't probe, especially since the work appeared to distract me from complaining about his Palo Alto apartment.

I texted back to tell him I was stuck in traffic, and not to worry, Maria was staying late. When he asked where I'd gone, I lied that I'd driven to Menlo Park to have coffee with an old colleague.

Next, I called Maria to tell her she could leave once Oli got home. I paused then, reluctant to say what had to be said.

Anything else? she asked.

Actually, yes. Would you mind not mentioning South San Francisco? Say you don't know where I went.

It was her turn to pause. Okay, she said, drawing out the last syllable.

What?

She hesitated. You always tell me where you're going and how long you'll be.

She was absolutely right. Okay, then will you tell him I drove to Menlo Park to meet a friend for coffee?

All right.

I felt like I owed her an explanation. I said, He knows I'm working part-time, but he doesn't think I get paid enough, so I don't want him to know how many hours I'm putting in.

Sure, all right. She never had questions.

I should have left it at that, but, silly me, the next morning, still feeling guilty about asking Maria to lie for me, I slipped an envelope with a fifty-dollar bill into her purse. Immediately, I felt better.

What's this for? she asked later, waving the envelope by her chin like a paper fan. She looked genuinely confused.

Just . . . thank you for telling Oli, you know, where I was.

Her face clouded. You don't have to pay me for that.

I know, I said quickly. It's a thank-you for everything. You've helped so much these past weeks by staying late with Henri.

You pay me overtime. She set the envelope on the kitchen island between us.

I slid it back to her. It's a small gesture of appreciation.

She cocked an eyebrow and muttered, Okay. Thanks.

After that Maria kept her distance. When I set out tea and cookies at the usual hour, she declined, saying she'd better run a load of laundry while she had the chance. Soon, we talked only about Henri and in a perfectly perfunctory manner. How much did he eat? What time did he poop? How long did he cry?

I fretted that she was growing dissatisfied with our family, and so, dipping into all that disposable income, I preemptively offered her a raise, which she accepted with the same suspicion, and which probably caused the further decline of our friendship.

LIKE I SAID, DETECTIVE, I took great pains to ensure that no one in my life had any clue what I was doing. Not only Oli and Maria, but also my friends Carla and Joanne. The one time the three of us finally managed to schedule an evening out, I stripped my new rose-gold Rolex off my wrist for fear of it raising questions.

Now that Joanne had a second child and Carla a serious boyfriend (this, on top of their already hectic careers as a VP at Banana Republic and an ob-gyn, respectively), we rarely got together. Back when Winnie had reappeared, we'd exchanged breathless witchy text messages, but I hadn't told them she'd become my friend, not to mention my boss.

I was the first to get to the bar. They arrived together, arm in arm, a few minutes later. Once they took their seats, their questions were rapid-fire: How different did Winnie look? How often did she come to San Francisco? Why on earth was I hanging out with her so much?

Thankfully, before I could answer that last question, our waiter delivered frothy cocktails in mismatched vintage glassware, and my friends paused to take long appreciative sips. It was then that Joanne noticed my amethyst Kelly, which I'd brought along at the last minute, figuring my friends would get a kick out of it.

Is that what I think it is? she asked, reaching for the bag.

It's a knockoff, I said quickly. I bought it in Hong Kong.

Purple! said Carla, who had no interest in designer fashion. How out of character. Have you ever, in your entire life, bought a purse that wasn't black?

Joanne deemed it a good copy before she spotted my zebra-print flats beneath the table. We don't see you for a couple of months and now you're a whole new person? She turned to Carla. How long have I been trying to get her to branch out and wear color?

Years, said Carla. Maybe decades.

They asked if I'd figured out what Winnie really did for work.

Joanne said, I bet it's something supershady. Import-export. Sanitation.

They laughed, and I laughed along.

Believe it or not, she was telling the truth, I said. She connects American leather goods companies to Chinese factories, and it's as boring as it sounds. I should know. I've been going over her contracts since I have some free time.

You have? Since when? Carla asked.

Do you think that's a good idea? said Joanne.

I assured them that I'd done my due diligence. After all, which one of us was the lawyer here?

The look they traded gave me a sense of all the text messages exchanged and lunches grabbed without me.

When they asked how Henri's preschool applications had gone, I merely answered, Great! We just need to make a final decision! Let's not discuss that. God knows I've wasted too much time on preschool already.

Joanne, whose two kids had attended one of the schools that had rejected us, nodded sympathetically. Later, I'd make up some bullshit story about how we'd had second thoughts about Divisadero Prep and managed to apply to Ming Liang at the last minute. And this is what Winnie had always known: as long as she could convince me to work for her, everything else would fall into place. The secrets I'd be forced to keep would alienate me from my loved ones, so that one day soon, I'd look around and find that the only one left to turn to was her.

Oh my god, said Joanne. We forgot to tell her.

Oh my god, Carla agreed. How was it not the first thing we mentioned?

Joanne's face flushed in excitement. She said that she'd run into Helena Sontag, our old classmate, at a conference, and learned that she taught at UVA from time to time, in the MBA program.

And? I said, my annoyance rising like baking dough.

Carla assured me this was all crucial background information. A couple years ago, Helena had been teaching a marketing class when Winnie walked in and asked to audit.

I said that made sense since she'd lived in Charlottesville for a couple years while caring for her aunt.

Exactly, said Joanne, by now so riled up the color had
spread down her neck. Except her aunt had already died
and Winnie was still living there—and here Joanne paused
for effect—because she was having an affair with her dead
aunt's husband.

That's how she got her green card, Carla practically
yelled, drawing looks from neighboring tables. By marrying her uncle.

Joanne turned to the gawking women at the neighboring table and clarified, No blood relation.

I tamped down my shock, not wanting to give my
friends that satisfaction. I tried to remember the man who'd
arrived at our dorm room with Winnie's aunt all those
years ago. The aunt I could conjure instantly. She'd worn
a blazer and scarf despite the unseasonable heat, as well
as an immense straw visor to shield her face from the sun.
The husband, though, had been unremarkable. An average
white man, neither tall nor short, fat nor thin. What had we
talked about over dinner at Fuki Sushi? He didn't eat raw
fish, that I recalled—odd, but not egregious for the standards of the time.

Is that not the grossest thing ever? Joanne said.

It speaks to who she is at her core, said Carla. She'll
stop at nothing to get what she wants.

Their salacious delivery of this gossip, their knowing
looks, their united front—all of it irritated me. I said some-

thing like, Maybe you don't grasp the value of American citizenship. Maybe it's something we all take for granted.

Ava, said Joanne. She married her aunt's husband. That's some Woody-Soon-Yi–level shit.

Don't get in too deep with her, said Carla. We don't know what she's capable of.

I swore that I was barely involved in her business, that I'd committed to nothing, and then swiftly moved on to the topic of our upcoming fifteenth college reunion. It was a full five months away, yet weekly emails were already arriving in our in-boxes, reminding us to register and book hotel rooms and submit pictures for the slide show.

I don't get why the fifteenth is a big deal, I said.

I'm going since I missed our tenth, said Joanne.

Carla said, If you both go, I'll go.

They looked at me. I shrugged noncommittally.

Do you think Winnie will come? asked Joanne.

Is she allowed to? Carla asked.

I said I didn't see why she would, especially since she wasn't in touch with anyone.

Except you, said Carla.

Joanne peered into the depths of her cocktail glass as though trying to divine a message in the leftover froth. It's so weird, her sudden reappearance, the way she sought you out.

Carla added, How the hell did she know Oli was a transplant surgeon? She isn't on social media, and you hadn't spoken to her in almost twenty years.

The alumni listserv, I said, before realizing that of course Winnie wouldn't have access to it, since she'd never graduated.

But Joanne and Carla had already moved on.

Make sure you ask her about the uncle-husband and report back, Joanne said, as Carla signaled for the waiter to bring another round.

I longed to call off the order, to get up and leave. I didn't want to spend another minute in that booth with these women, my oldest, closest friends.

You see, Detective, that's how deep in I was. Instead of being repulsed by Winnie's marriage to Bertrand Lewis, I held my friends' wholly natural reaction to it against them. In fact, in my sick and addled mind, I admired Winnie for once again saying, To hell with the haters, I'm going to do what I have to do. That level of audacity, daring, nerve— well, it was intoxicating.

10

That June, six months after Winnie had first reached out to me, Boss Mak arrived in Palo Alto for a few days of consultations and tests with Oli and the rest of the Stanford transplant team. Winnie went along to translate as well as to provide moral support.

She told me she'd been shocked to see him at the airport, his face gaunt, his blazer hanging off his shrunken frame. He'd stopped going to the office and, as far as Winnie could tell, he spent his days watching convoluted K-dramas with plots too difficult to recount. He didn't even have the strength to complain about his daughter, who'd taken over the factories—a pretty, pampered only child, who'd attended the best schools in the world and yet, according to him, somehow lacked all common sense.

Once Oli received Boss Mak's test results, he told him the transplant committee would discuss his case and give him an answer in a few weeks, making sure to emphasize how difficult it was to take on foreigners as patients. To this, Boss Mak nodded sagely and said (with Winnie translating), I appreciate your taking the time to consider my situation, nonetheless. I'd like to make a donation of half a million dollars to the hospital to support your very good work.

Now, as you probably know, Detective, ironclad protocols and endless wait lists govern liver transplants in the US, so much so that when Winnie first told me about Boss Mak, I said he'd be better off staying in China, which, I knew from Oli, had a plethora of available livers that were rumored to have come from executed political prisoners. But Winnie explained that like all wealthy people in China, Boss Mak would never voluntarily subject himself to the country's subpar medical system. He demanded the very best.

When I repeated what I'd absorbed from Oli about the extreme organ shortages all across the country and the near ban on transplants for foreigners following the election, the smile that played on Winnie's lips was mocking. Everyone knows there are ways to skirt the rules, she said. Didn't I recall what had happened at the UCLA Medical Center, where four Yakuza bosses had jetted in from Tokyo to claim pristine new livers, the transplants performed by the chair of the department himself? Sure, eventually the *L.A. Times* did a big exposé, questioning how these foreign gangsters had jumped the line, but what really came of it? The chair remained the chair; the Yakuza kept their livers.

Was I surprised that Winnie would go to such lengths to help Boss Mak? I can't say that I was, Detective. After all, he was the closest thing she had to family. Her parents barely spoke to her; her aunt in Virginia was dead.

Do I believe the rupture with her parents pushed her into a life of crime? Yes, I suppose so. Don't the parents always bear at least some of the blame? From what I could gather, her estrangement from her parents happened in two distinct phases, over a period of fifteen years. The first was when she'd had to drop out of Stanford. It was too dangerous to tell her parents the truth—Chinese students were hiring expensive lawyers to fight the threat of prison sentences—but how else could she explain such a sudden departure? She studied the problem from every angle and concluded she had no choice except to say she'd flunked out.

Waiting to board the plane at SFO, she called them from a pay phone at the gate. Later she'd tell me how torturous it was to say the words, especially when she pictured her schoolmates whiling away the hours tossing plastic balls into cups of beer and racking up B's. It's true, at our illustrious institution, grade inflation was a joke. I don't think it would have been possible to flunk out unless you really put your mind to it. Luckily, unlike universities in China, Stanford didn't send grade reports to parents, so hers never got to see the neat row of A's she'd earned—yes, even in Writing and Rhetoric. (All the writing tutors at the library had known her by name.)

Following seventeen-plus hours of flying, the long wait for the bus, the hot and dusty ride home, when she finally wrestled her suitcases up the stairs to the apartment, her father wouldn't come out of his room. Her mother pointed to the table where a few bowls sat beneath a mesh cover. For a few minutes she watched Winnie shovel food into her mouth and then said, Don't tell anyone why you came back. Just say you couldn't pay the fees. She rose and went to join her husband in the bedroom.

Winnie was so hungry she ate all the tofu in its congealed brown sauce, the soggy mustard greens, the cold hardened rice. Through the wall she heard the rise and fall of the television, her mother's titter, her father's grunt. Three months she'd been gone, and they couldn't even look at her.

She applied off cycle to Xiamen University. The school made an exception and accepted her, thanks to her stellar high school grades, as well as the prestigious government scholarship that had enabled her to go abroad in the first place. Probably they also felt sorry for her.

You're the girl who had to leave Stanford, professors and students alike would say. What was it like over there?

She told me her answer varied depending on her mood. It was paradise, she said to her plump, eager lab mate. The campus was so beautiful, it was like biking through a Hollywood movie.

Honestly it wasn't so great, she said to the gangly, nervous economics TA. If I could do it over, I'd have applied to Oxbridge. More intellectually rigorous. Cheaper, too.

As soon as there was available space, she moved into the

dorms. She told me the other students were always amazed to discover she was local, so rarely did she go home.

THE SECOND AND FINAL PHASE of Winnie's rupture with her parents happened years later, after she'd divorced Bertrand Lewis. Her parents had been quite understandably enraged when she'd married him for a green card, so she found it strange that they seemed equally upset when she left him.

After drinks that day with Carla and Joanne, I questioned Winnie about Bertrand. She told me to put aside my preconceived notions about the kind of man who'd marry his late wife's niece. She claimed that Bert had been nothing but loyal and loving to her aunt. In fact, she believed it was his devastation at losing her that drove him to accept Winnie's proposal.

The afternoon they drove back from their City Hall ceremony, he shyly popped open a bottle of cheap champagne. It made her cringe. She knew she should put an end to the nonsense then and there, but he looked so hopeful in his good sports coat that she sat down and polished off the whole bottle with him. She was in no mood to cook, so, for dinner, they scarfed down Ruffles potato chips dipped in ranch dressing. It was late when they rose from the table. Her eyelids were heavy, and all she wanted was to lay her cheek on a warm chest. Foolishly, she let him lead her into the main bedroom. She never went in there, always leaving his clean laundry in a neat pile on the recliner in front of the television. He hadn't bothered to put away the clothes, and the sight of them heaped onto one side of the king-size bed irked her. Why had she wasted time folding every last pair of his briefs? He swept the laundry onto the carpet and grinned, which would have irritated her further, except he looked so delighted with himself that she caught a glimpse of the boy he must have been. And so, she slid out of her jeans and darted beneath the covers, where at least it was cozy and snug.

In the middle of the night, she returned to the pullout couch in the study. She was quick to clarify that once she'd told him how she felt, he never pressured her to sleep with him again. He gave her a place to live for the next three years while she waited for her green card, auditing business school classes at UVA, taking whatever under-the-table work she could find. After a babysitting client requested that she speak only Mandarin to her infant daughter, Winnie started offering her services as a Chinese tutor. This won't surprise you, Detective: within a year, she'd transformed Bert's finished basement into an after-school Chinese program for the city's elite. Business executives, doctors, lawyers, academics, all sent their kids, ages two to eighteen.

But no matter how busy Winnie was with her work, she held up her side of the deal with Bert. She cleaned the toilets, did the shopping, cooked tasty and nutritious meals. The day her green card arrived, Bert took her to an Italian restaurant to celebrate.

Over a shared slice of tiramisu, his eyes moistened. I've

enjoyed your company, he said. It's going to be lonely without you.

She moved into an apartment of her own after that, though she continued renting Bert's basement for her tutoring business. And who knows how long she would have stayed in Charlottesville if not for the election? On top of her disappointment with the president-elect, she said she'd grown bored of teaching basic Chinese-language classes and had begun to resent what she described as the menacingly friendly ways of the South. As such, she planned a long vacation to China to visit her parents, whom she hadn't seen in eight years, and to explore the idea of moving home for good.

Stepping into the entryway of her childhood apartment, though, with its flickering ceiling light and peeling paint, Winnie said she knew she'd made a terrible mistake. Five consecutive weeks she spent in that cramped space, sharing a single bathroom with her mother and father, plus the occasional silent meal. By the time she met Boss Mak, on that trip to Guangzhou with her cousin and her cousin's friends, she'd sunk into a deep malaise. She dreaded opening her eyes each morning; she'd forgotten what it was like to actually be interested in what someone had to say.

Lying in Boss Mak's arms in that hotel room, she clung to his words, asking questions late into the night, about growth opportunities for his factories and the demands of working with international brands.

He said, You're too smart to be stuck in Xiamen. Go to Beijing or Shanghai. I can make some introductions.

The truth was Winnie couldn't stand those cities: smog so thick you went weeks without seeing the sun, crowds so dense you lost entire days waiting in queues.

Boss Mak laughed, his chest gently jostling her head, and said, I see you're American now. In that case, why waste your time in China?

This, she later told me, was exactly what she'd needed to hear. Within weeks, she'd purchased her plane ticket to Los Angeles and told her parents she'd made up her mind to remain in America.

At last her father raised his eyes from his rice bowl and looked her full in the face. It's for the best, he said, and then retired to his room, leaving Winnie and her mother to clear the dirty dishes.

She boarded that plane knowing she would never again have a home to return to in China. She was free. Free to make a life for herself, to do as she saw fit. And, Detective, I cannot overstate how rare that was for someone like Winnie, the only child of Chinese parents. So, you asked if the estrangement had anything to do with her eventual career path? Yes, it's quite clear it did.

Still, no one following the events leading up to Winnie's departure would have guessed that within months, she'd be back in her homeland buying up counterfeit handbags. That the Sheraton Dongguan and the Shangri-La Shenzhen, and the Marriott Guangzhou would become, in a sense, her second homes.

She told me that the last time she saw Boss Mak healthy was right after she submitted her application for American citizenship. They were in the clubhouse of his country club in Dongguan, sipping cool drinks after a round of golf. By then they were business partners and appeared freely together in public. His disease had not yet progressed, and he looked tanned and strong, so she held her tongue when he downed his beer and ordered another. She had other things on her mind. If her citizenship application was accepted, she'd be stuck in the US until her new passport came through, and she was pondering a quick visit to Xiamen to see her parents. Did Boss Mak think she should go?

Ever measured, he replied, It depends on your motivations.

What Winnie wanted more than anything was to rub her success in her parents' faces. Maybe the soft chairs and the starched tablecloths and the cold, tart lemonade in that over-air-conditioned clubhouse had something to do with this, but all at once she was furious that they'd believed her when she'd told them she'd flunked out of Stanford. Didn't they know their own daughter? Didn't they know her capabilities? Why hadn't they pushed to find out what was truly going on?

And then she tried to imagine how they would have responded if she'd told them what she'd done. Their reaction would have been the same—anger, disgust, and above all, shame. She couldn't have trusted them to protect her if it had come down to that. Because after all the hoopla—the fancy awards ceremony, the write-up in the *Xiamen Daily*, the glorious send-off organized by her high school— she'd humiliated them by dropping out, and that was unforgivable.

That's when she revealed to Boss Mak that as a high school senior she'd won a national scholarship and been accepted to Stanford. Until then, all he'd known was that she'd graduated top of her class at Xiamen University.

He set down his empty glass. Why didn't you go?

I did, she said, for one quarter. Less than three months. She let slip a bitter laugh.

When she'd recounted the whole saga, he pulled out his handkerchief and dabbed his face, overcome. He said, I wish I'd known you back then. I think I could have convinced them to let you stay.

She didn't point out that all this had happened years ago, in a different era, when there was zero sympathy for the students involved. Even the son of the Party secretary of Tianjin had been expelled from Harvard.

What he said next would stay with her.

You were a child who was desperate. And you were clearly as smart as everyone else there. That has to count for something.

In the end, she told me, she didn't go home to Xiamen. Instead, she wired an obscene amount of money into her mother's bank account. Her mother accepted the transfer but didn't otherwise acknowledge the gift.

So, no, Detective, I can't say that Winnie's determination to help Boss Mak get his transplant and save his life surprised me, but then again, neither did her reversal.

11

While Boss Mak languished in bed in Dongguan, awaiting Oli and the committee's decision, his daughter, the former senior VP of Mak International, settled into her new role as its acting president. Armed with a Wharton MBA, a wardrobe of smartly off-kilter Vivienne Westwood suits, and her father's unwavering support, Mandy Mak introduced a steady stream of initiatives, from restructuring assembly lines into small teams of workers for maximum flexibility to issuing sharp new uniforms to boost morale. But her biggest innovation was implemented not in the Maks' legitimate factories, but in our counterfeits business.

In Winnie's original scheme, we were constantly on the defense, playing catch-up with the brands. Once a new style hit a boutique, we raced to track down a black factory in Guangzhou that could get a hold of that handbag, take it apart, source the necessary materials, and train their workers to perfectly re-create each component. Naturally, this took time. And because counterfeits factories were routinely raided and shut down, we constantly had to seek out new partners.

The solution that Mandy Mak laid out to Winnie over the phone was as simple as it was risky. The Maks' legitimate factories already produced handbags for all the biggest brands, so instead of running two separate businesses, one legitimate and one less so, she proposed they *counterfeit their own brands*, right there on the premises. Why not build their own black factory nearby? Genuine samples and blueprints could pass through the back door into the hands of our associates, enabling replicas to be released at the same time as their real counterparts, a veritable coup.

Now, Detective, I know what you're thinking. Wouldn't the black factory eat into the profits of the legitimate one? The answer is no, not necessarily. Generally speaking, the customer who drops a couple hundred dollars for a one-to-one is not at all the same person who pays upward of two thousand dollars for the real thing. Mandy Mak wouldn't be cannibalizing her legitimate factories but growing her family's handbag empire as a whole. All she had to do was make sure the international brands never, ever found out.

To be clear, the whole plan was outrageous, truly outrageous. I couldn't fathom why Winnie had bothered to recount it to me instead of rejecting it outright. The international brands, already skittish about manufacturing their goods in China, yet unable to walk away from the cheap labor, implemented harsh regulations to combat IP theft. Leftover materials had to be accounted for down to the millimeter; blueprints were stored in industrial safes, factory rejects swiftly destroyed.

But when I attempted to warn Winnie about the riskiness of this new venture, to express the opinion that had Boss Mak been in better health, he'd have roundly rejected this move, she replied with a smirk and said, I've never seen him turn down money, and this is a hell of a lot of it. She quickly came to the conclusion that I had to go to Dongguan to work out the details of this new partnership, one that would make the Maks our sole supplier of counterfeit handbags.

I argued that the plan was too dangerous, that the Maks could never pull it off, that Winnie was giving up too much power, and all for something that was doomed to fail.

I even tried to appeal to her ego. This was your ingenious scheme, I said. You're the one who made this all happen. And now, if they control the supply chain, you're at their mercy. You work for them.

Frankly, Detective, I can't say for sure if I truly bought into my own arguments, or if I was just grasping for reasons to decline the trip. Because even then I knew what it meant: to go to Dongguan would be to become Winnie's proxy, to leap from employee to partner, equally accountable, equally culpable, equally entangled with the Maks and their numerous other illegitimate schemes.

And so I tried to buy myself some time, suggesting we take a few weeks to consider our options, but Winnie wouldn't hear of it. She swept an arm through the air, as though that could vanquish all my concerns.

No, she said. I didn't get this far by playing it safe. We're in.

Desperate, I told her I couldn't leave Henri.

In a tone laced with disdain, she said. Come on, not this again.

Oli will never let me go. You know how he is.

Her expression hardened. Well, if you can't talk to him, I can. In fact, I can tell him everything. Is that what you want?

The skin on the back of my neck prickled. I searched her face for any traces of humor or irony—surely, she was kidding. Surely, she was a split second away from barking out a laugh. Instead, I found only pure distilled scorn. In that moment I saw Winnie for who she truly was: not an awkward bookworm, nor a brilliant iconoclast, but a common thug.

I said, All right. When should I leave?

She clapped her hands, instantly returned to her old cheerful self. The shift was dizzying.

We'll get you on the next flight out. It'll be great, you'll see. As though she hadn't just threatened to ruin me, my marriage, my life.

THAT EVENING, WHEN OLI WALKED through the door, weary and depleted, as he always was at the end of the week, I was ready to press my case. His favorite boeuf bourguignon—the only thing I'd ever learned to cook—simmered on the stove; four kinds of hard and soft cheeses and an assortment of water crackers were fanned out across the walnut board; a good red Burgundy beckoned from the decanter.

I served my husband a steaming helping of the rich, dark stew. The meat was tender, the shallots fragrant, the mushrooms glossy as pearls. He inched his chair to mine and laid his head on my shoulder. I pressed the pads of my fingers into his scalp and he practically purred.

That was when I told him about the trip.

His head launched up like a basketball. Shenzhen, China? Day after tomorrow?

I reminded him that Winnie couldn't leave the country because of her citizenship application and I was the only lawyer on staff. I heard the words leave my mouth and fail to make sense, so I babbled on and on. But since I couldn't reveal the real reason for the trip, all Oli could gather was that I was jetting off once again, at the last minute, and worse, leaving our son behind.

Ava, tell me the truth, are you having an affair? he asked.

The piece of meat in my mouth turned to gristle and I spat it into my napkin.

Your hair, he said, gesturing at my new auburn highlights, and those colorful dresses, it's so fucking cliché.

I swore I was faithful; he was the one who'd always chided me to wear more color, I did it for him! I tried to explain that business in China had to be done face-to-face, that I would shake some hands and sign some stuff and turn around and fly right back, oh, except that my grandmother was turning ninety this week, and for once in my life I'd be able to celebrate with her, and surely he could grant me that much?

What's come over you? he asked. Can you hear how bizarre you sound right now?

I shut my mouth.

Oli pushed aside his plate. Our son's being raised by his nanny.

Now this was too much. My carefully laid-out argument splintered like a log. I roared back, And that's my fault? Coming from a man who lives apart from his family for the majority of the week?

You know the kind of hours I'm working, Oli said, his voice cracking. This'll be the first day off I've had in three weeks.

Here the regular me, the *real* me, would have caught myself, would have stopped and listened. The possessed me charged on, thinking only of herself.

Oh, come now, you knew what you were getting into. No one forced you.

He blanched. Fine. Pay Maria to stay the entire time you're gone. I can't drive back and forth from Palo Alto every night.

I'm glad your priorities are so clear. I stormed around the room searching for my phone so I could send Maria a message, offer another raise.

He said, You're the one upending our lives with this so-called job. For christ's sake, I don't even know what it is you do.

That's because you never listen, I yelled from the kitchen, where my phone had been resting precariously close to the sink. I've told you a half dozen times, but all you do is work, work, work and then come home on the weekend and spend fifteen minutes here and there playing with your son. You call that parenting?

In lieu of a response there was a deafening crash. I ran back to the dining room where, in a highly uncharacteristic move, Oli had swept the Baccarat crystal vase that had been a gift from his mother off the sideboard and onto the floor.

He stood there with his head in his hands, shoulders heaving with each breath. A lifetime ago I would have taken him in my arms, nestled my face into the warm hollow beneath his chin. Instead, I told him, Clean that up before you leave, and walked out of the room.

THREE DAYS AFTER WINNIE FIRST proposed and then ordered me on this trip, I landed at the Shenzhen airport in the middle of a deluge. I was lamenting my failure to pack an umbrella when I caught sight of my name on a placard, held by a young man in a budget suit with stylishly shaggy collar-length hair.

Despite my protests, he wrested my Rollaboard from me and dashed into the downpour beneath a capacious black golf umbrella, promising to return with the car.

A while later, I stepped outside and was instantly shrink-wrapped in humidity for the fleeting moment before I slid

into the gleaming silver Mercedes, chilled to the temperature of a walk-in refrigerator. The leather seat was stiff and
unyielding, the icy bottled water in the cup holder so cold
it made my teeth ache. When I typed the Wi-Fi password
taped above the door handle into my phone, a picture of a
sleeping Henri arrived from Maria, the sweat-matted hair
plastered to his forehead, a sure sign he'd been crying. The
guilt that gushed through me was a viscous, toxic sludge. I
checked my email to see if Oli had written, but he had not.

Traffic slowed to a standstill, and the driver explained
that flooding had closed one of the highway lanes. Outside
my hermetically sealed box, a couple on a motorcycle, clad
in makeshift rain ponchos fashioned from garbage bags,
squinted miserably into the storm. A red-faced man in a
tiny electric car leaned on the horn and then lowered his
window and hacked out a wad of phlegm.

I popped in my earbuds and pulled up a Chinese pod-
cast on my phone to get the language in my head, which
would have made Winnie scoff. Stop worrying, she'd
chided. You're not there to have deep conversations, you're
there to demonstrate that we care enough about this partnership to show up in person. For once you don't have to be
the top student. Just get on that plane and go.

Was I surprised she was back to cracking jokes as
though we were old friends again? Not really, Detective.
You'd know better than I—isn't that the mark of a successful gangster? Utterly charming and utterly ruthless from
one moment to the next?

Case in point, in that car, I stretched out my legs and listened to a strikingly charismatic ex–con man explain how
he'd convinced Chinese housewives to hire him to murder
their cheating husbands so that he could abscond with their
life savings.

The next time I opened my eyes, the rain had cleared, and
pale streams of light battled through the clouds. The car
stopped before a gate that slid back to let us through. The
driver drove up to the factory's main entrance, parked, and
hurried around to open my door.

A tall man with a prematurely receding hairline bounded
down a short flight of stairs to greet me. He was dressed
more casually than the driver in a tight Prada polo shirt. In
rapid, Chinese-accented English he said, Hello! I'm Kaiser
Shih, deputy manager of Mak International. How was your
flight? You flew in from San Francisco, right? I just got
back from L.A. last week. It's my favorite city in America.
Well, after Las Vegas, of course.

He led me through the glass doors and into an elevator that deposited us before a bright, tastefully furnished
conference room. A young woman with a ballerina bun
sat at the head of the table, rapidly thumbing a phone in
a Goyard-monogrammed case. She was none other than
Mandy Mak. Dressed in one of her trademark suits, with
an asymmetrical neckline and a full, knife-pleated skirt,
paired with shiny red patent stilettos that perfectly matched
her lipstick, she looked like a movie star playing a CEO in
a Hollywood rom-com. Next to her was a plump man in a

threadbare shirt, which contrasted starkly with the thick rope of gold ringing his squat neck. This, Kaiser Shih told me, was Manager Chiang, head of the new counterfeits factory.

Introductions were made. I asked after Boss Mak, and Mandy stunned me by throwing her arms around me and thanking me for arranging the appointment with Oli and the transplant team.

In contrast, Manager Chiang soberly shook my hand.

I told him I'd heard great things about his work.

Not at all, not at all, he replied.

He's being modest, said Mandy. Do you know why his replicas are so good? He managed to hire a floor chief from Dior's main factory here.

The man said mildly, That is true.

We sat down at the table and went through the motions of finalizing the terms of our new agreement, after which another round of handshakes ensued.

Manager Chiang excused himself to get to another meeting.

Came from nothing, Kaiser Shih told me. Dropped out of school in the fifth grade and worked his way up—the Chinese dream.

Mandy had to leave soon after that to catch a flight to Milan for a trade show, but not before instructing Kaiser Shih to show me around the premises.

I'm sorry to miss the dinner tonight, she said, but Kaiser Shih and the others will take good care of you. Enjoy!

Have a glass of champagne for me! She swished out of the room on her four-inch heels.

Kaiser Shih led me through a pair of glass doors beyond which some of the world's finest handbags were made. The rooms were pristine and well-ventilated, giving the rows of uniformed workers—young women, all of them, with their hair pulled back beneath hairnets, their mouths and noses shielded by medical-grade masks—the precise, efficient air of surgical nurses.

In the samples room, he held up a fifties-style frame bag in bottle-green glazed leather and told me, Marc Jacobs, Spring 2020, dropping next year.

As the tour progressed, I studied irregularly shaped panels of leather laid out across tabletops like antique maps. I watched workers stitch Tory Burch labels into patterned clutches, those navy-blue twin T's that, by now, I knew by heart. Turning a corner, I nearly walked into a rack of Prada Saffiano leather totes, hanging there as casually as whole roasted ducks in a Chinatown window.

Facetiously Kaiser Shih said, Tell no one you saw these, or Prada will have my neck. He had an infectious laugh, resonant and flowing like a sudden surge of water from a tap.

Maybe it was dehydration from the long flight, or mild poisoning from the deadly Chinese smog that the Western press constantly lamented, or maybe it was psychological— my slowly burgeoning guilt breaking through the layers of rationalization. Whatever the case, my head began to throb. I grew wobbly and fatigued. Following Kaiser Shih up yet another staircase, the toe of my shoe caught on some minuscule overhang, and down I went.

I'm so sorry! he said. Are you all right?

I said I felt completely out of it and perhaps the pollution was to blame.

Could be, he said. Foreigners always complain about it. He gazed at me with such pity and tenderness that I wondered if we might be different species—he, so healthy and resilient, I, so vulnerable and weak.

He suggested taking me back to the hotel to rest, but I insisted on seeing the counterfeits factory; after all, I'd come all this way.

Outside, the clouds had dispersed, and the noonday sun hit me full in the face. We crossed the courtyard, skirting puddles, and followed a narrow path through a thick cove of trees to a small concrete structure at the very edge of the compound, hidden away from the eyes of international and local inspectors alike. In contrast to the rest of the buildings, this one needed a paint job, and its windows were marred by iron bars, thick curtains.

Once inside, I saw the giant nets strung across the stairwells, as though for a circus trapeze.

What's all this? I asked, and then the answer came to me.

Worker safety, Kaiser Shih said.

My stomach roiled.

We climbed to the top floor and he pulled out a ring of keys and unlocked a heavy door. Here we are.

The room that opened up before me was blisteringly hot, though the women at the sewing machines, many inexplicably clad in long sleeves, appeared oblivious to the temperature. One or two of the women, past middle age, with more white in their hair than black, glanced my way, then returned to pushing flaps of glazed bottle-green leather across their machines.

You see? Kaiser Shih said, pointing. Ours will be ready as soon as Marc's.

A corner of the room was reserved for an office, and someone waved at me from one of the desks. It was Ah Seng, the man who had taken me to that creepy apartment building back in January. As I returned his wave, a girl in the opposite corner of the room caught my eye. She couldn't have been older than fourteen, and when she raised a handkerchief to mop the sweat at her hairline, I saw that her first two fingers were missing. I tasted acid in the back of my throat. My struggle to breathe in the thick swampy air was exacerbated by the fleece blankets tacked over each window. I'd naively mistaken them for curtains from down below.

Kaiser Shih touched my elbow and asked, All right?

I swallowed hard. He waved over the foreman, formerly of Dior, a lanky man with pockmarked cheeks.

Meet Ms. Wong from America, Kaiser Shih said.

The foreman held out his five-fingered hand, and when I reached for it, my body rebelled and listed to one side.

Somehow Kaiser Shih caught me and held me upright.

Ah Seng rushed over with a tin cup of water, which Kaiser Shih pushed away, shouting, Get her bottled water. She's a foreigner.

He helped me into the corridor, where it was significantly cooler. With my back pressed to the wall, I let gravity take my seat to the ground. Inside that infernal room, the whirring machinery never slowed.

Ah Seng returned with a bottle of water, which I gulped down.

I'll drive you to the hotel, Kaiser Shih said.

There's a driver, I managed to get out.

Then I'll accompany you there.

In the car, he told the driver to turn up the air-conditioning and then trained the vents on me.

How can they work like that? I asked.

What do you mean? said Kaiser Shih.

It's way too hot.

They're used to it.

It's inhumane.

He snorted. It's much, much better than many I've seen. His gaze skimmed over me. Winnie didn't tell you?

I knew I should stop, but I couldn't help myself. How old was the girl in the corner?

What girl?

The one missing two fingers. Twelve? Thirteen?

He made a sound halfway between a sigh and a groan. Ava, he said, if those girls could get legitimate work, why would they be there?

To this I had no answer.

The car pulled up to the Sheraton, a 1970s-era circular monstrosity the color of an overcooked salmon fillet.

Get some rest, he said. Your driver will pick you up for dinner.

In the cavernous atrium, the hotel receptionist assured me that my Chinese was good for an American and came out from behind the desk to personally escort me up to my top-floor junior suite. She droned on about the wrap-around views of this grimy, smog-enveloped industrial city, the complicated system of light switches and dimmers on the wall, the complimentary platter of pears and apples and mangoes, carved to resemble local flora and fauna. At last she left, and I chucked every last apple-swan into the trash (a precaution I always took in China, along with boiling water in an electric kettle to brush my teeth). I lowered the thermostat, drew the blackout drapes, and slid into the bed. A dozen tiny fists pounded at my temples, and when I touched the back of my hand to my forehead, it burned. My body screamed for me to break loose, while my brain retorted that it was too late. I'd scrawled my name across that contract; I'd shaken each and every hand. People like these, with their money and their contacts and their illicit dealings, did not take kindly to being crossed. Hadn't Winnie herself turned on me the instant I dared rebel?

AT THE DESIGNATED HOUR, I trudged out into the still-hot day to meet my driver, who ferried me to another of Dongguan's large luxury hotels. My strategy was to be supremely affable and uninteresting; I would get through the evening without asking inconvenient questions, without pissing anyone off. The elevator disgorged me into a palatial rooftop restaurant with brushed-gold walls and a mirrored ceiling inlaid with bronze dragons. I was led to a massive private room that could have easily sat fifty, but which currently contained a single table in the very center, around which sat three ordinary-looking men in dark blazers and one young woman.

Recognizing the woman's ballerina bun, I cried out, Mandy, I thought you were in Milan.

The woman turned. It was not Mandy, but another young woman in a tight black bandage dress, accessorized with a heavy gold chain-link necklace. Two of the men chuckled uncomfortably, and the third said, This is Linlin, my girlfriend.

Despite both Winnie's and Oli's descriptions, I could not reconcile Boss Mak's thick head of silver hair and well-groomed mustache with the sickly yellowish cast of his skin and eyes, with the way his thin shoulders swam within his jacket.

I ducked my head, mortified, and apologized to the girlfriend, who didn't seem offended, and then I took Boss Mak's hand. I hadn't expected him to be well enough to come.

His grip remained commanding. He said, How could I miss the chance to meet you in person? Please thank your husband again for his time.

The other men introduced themselves. The one with the sly eyes and the garish orange tie was the recently appointed vice mayor of Guangzhou. Clearly, Boss Mak had strategically invited him to invest in our business. The older jowly man with the jet-black comb-over was the retired police chief, who received a monthly retainer in exchange for keeping all necessary parties abreast of scheduled raids.

The vice mayor cheerfully warned me that none of them spoke English, while the police chief leaned over and poured me a glass of white wine—a Burgundy grand cru.

Everyone clinked glasses and sang gan bei, including Boss Mak, who drank with almost exaggerated gusto, perhaps anticipating that if Oli agreed to take him on as a patient, he'd be required to abstain from alcohol for at least six months.

Despite the Advil I'd downed earlier, my temples throbbed like stereo speakers. I took small sips of my wine whenever pressed and hoped they'd be satisfied.

After his initial introduction, Boss Mak spoke sparingly, perhaps to preserve his energy. He all but ignored Linlin, who refilled his glass and asked if he felt chilly and wanted the air-conditioning turned down, and then, when he said no, wound a camel cashmere scarf around his neck. If anything, she seemed to be more nurse than mistress, and I couldn't decide which was worse.

Very quickly we ran out of topics commensurate with my language ability, so I was relieved when the door to the room swung open and in walked Kaiser Shih, still dressed in the same Prada polo in lieu of a blazer.

Hello, hi, sorry I'm late, Kaiser Shih said in English.

The police chief, whose complexion glowed crimson with drink, said, At last our English expert has arrived.

Boss Mak wagged a finger at Kaiser Shih, though he spoke to me. As you probably already know, my deputy manager here talks way too much, but since I don't know English, I only have to listen to about fifty percent of what he says.

Kaiser Shih accepted the ribbing with good-natured resignation. He asked if I was feeling better, and I lied that I was.

The vice mayor called for the waitstaff to serve the food and to open another bottle of white Burgundy. When a waitress approached with the wine, the vice mayor seized it from her, filled Kaiser Shih's glass to the brim and said, in English, Bottoms up.

Bottoms up, the police chief cried. You're the youngest and the tallest so you must drink the most.

Dutifully Kaiser Shih raised the glass to his lips and downed the pricey wine in one long pull, while the two men cheered him on. They reminded me of the first-year associates at my old firm—type A about everything including partying.

Now you two, Kaiser Shih said, filling the other men's glasses. You, too, Ava, he said, pointing at me.

Weakly, I lifted my glass. A hint of menace hung over

the festivities, as though at any moment, the mood might swerve from jubilant to belligerent.

Meanwhile, Boss Mak observed the proceedings with a distant amused expression, like a king gazing upon his subjects from a high perch. Each time his wineglass touched his lips, I pictured his scarred liver, shrunken and hardened, unable to clear the toxins building up within. Oli had once showed me a picture of a pair of livers, one healthy and one damaged. The good organ was smooth and pliant and a deep glowing red; the bad one pallid, rigid, brutally marred. Boss Mak looked at least a decade older than my mom, even though they'd have both been seventy. And yet here he was, being fussed over by this pretty, young woman, while what remained of my mother sat in an urn on the living room mantel of my childhood home.

The first dish arrived, a cold appetizer plate with crunchy jellyfish and thinly sliced marbled ham and fat nuggets of smoked goose. Then double-boiled sharks' fin soup. Then abalone with baby bok choy, crispy fried grouper, lacquered slices of Peking duck, all accompanied by more wine, this time a red Bordeaux.

Kaiser Shih ensured my plate was always full, repeatedly asking if I was enjoying the food. In truth, every morsel was too greasy and overseasoned, crossing the line from decadent to debauched.

The police chief and the vice mayor told loud stories in Cantonese—which I tried in vain to follow—that ended in backslapping, wild guffaws. They debated the handicapping tip sheets for upcoming races at the Macau Jockey Club, where they all appeared to be members. Linlin stifled a yawn and excused herself to go to the bathroom, and I wished I could get up and follow. But what would I say to her? What could we possibly have in common besides both wishing to be elsewhere?

The waitress brought bowls of chilled honeydew sago and a platter of cut fruits (which I awkwardly declined). Linlin returned to the table with fresh lipstick, and I suspected she must have sat on the commode scrolling through her phone to pass the time. Once the men had finished their dessert, the vice mayor ordered a round of cognac, a glass of which they forced on me.

A toast, he said. To new partnerships and new profits!

Everyone shouted, Gan bei!

My head spun in sluggish circles. Each blink was a battle to raise my eyelids. The waitress entered clutching the leather check holder, and I straightened, momentarily buoyed by having had the foresight to hand my credit card to the maître d' upon arrival.

But instead of bringing me the check, the waitress went to Boss Mak.

They know me here, he said, scrawling his name on the receipt. They'd never let you pay.

I told them Winnie had insisted.

Boss Lady can pay the next time she comes, said the police chief, whose skin tone by this point had darkened to maroon.

All at once I remembered the red envelopes I'd brought in my purse. I passed them out with both hands, saying, A small token from me and Fang Wenyi.

Boss Mak reached underneath the table and brought out an enormous shopping bag in that unmistakable shade of orange. And a present from us to you.

This, I hadn't anticipated. I'd brought no other gifts and didn't know what to do.

Open it, said the vice mayor.

Yes, urged Kaiser Shih and the police chief.

Even Linlin perked up.

The vice mayor asked the waitress to clear the dirty glasses, and she went one step further and laid clean white napkins over the soiled tablecloth. I set down the lightly grained orange box, undid the brown grosgrain ribbon, and folded back layers of white tissue.

A gasp escaped me. Nestled in the box was a rare crocodile Birkin 25, the color of merlot, of rubies, of blood. The men beamed at me, pleased with my astonishment. Linlin's red-lacquered finger inched toward the bag. Boss Mak swatted her away.

I held the Birkin up to the chandelier. It seemed to pulse like a living, breathing thing. From every angle it appeared authentic, worth at least forty thousand dollars.

My vision blurred. I blinked a couple times. How did you get this?

Boss Mak said, I have a contact at the Zurich boutique.

He winked. Even if ninety-nine percent of people can't tell the difference between a real and a superfake, we can.

The bag was worth ten times the cash in all the red envelopes combined. That's when I grasped just how determined Boss Mak was to join that transplant list. He smiled serenely at me, the very picture of a man who always got what he wanted.

Another toast, cried the vice mayor, who had at some point refilled our glasses. To friendships, old and new!

Gan bei, gan bei, gan bei!

After the cognac bottle had been emptied, we stood and gathered our things and rode the elevator to the ground floor. Linlin helped Boss Mak into the back of his Range Rover. I was scanning the parking lot for my driver when the police chief said, It's not yet eleven, let's hit the KTV lounge.

My eyes watered. I could have fallen asleep right there on the ground. I had to get up early to drive to Hong Kong for my grandma's birthday. I said, I drank too much, I have jet lag, please, I can barely stand.

But they didn't care. Kaiser Shih's large hand clamped onto my wrist and pulled me along, saying he'd already texted my driver and sent him home. Someone pushed me into a roomy SUV, and I lay back, grateful for a place to rest my head.

Minutes later Kaiser Shih nudged me awake and guided me out of the car. A high-speed elevator spirited us skyward to a swanky lounge with sumptuous velvet couches and low mahogany tables scattered beneath fluorescent purple lights. The host led us to a private room with a pair of generous sofas facing a screen that filled the entire wall. Above our heads glinted a mini disco ball.

While the police chief passed out cigars, I went in search of the restroom and then to the bar for a double espresso, which the bemused bartender slid toward me. When I returned to the group, a waiter was setting down bottles of Dom Pérignon and Johnnie Walker Blue Label and yet another complimentary fruit platter. A treacly string intro filled the air, and the vice mayor sang tenderly about the lover who had walked out the door without so much as a glance. He had a pleasant baritone voice, warm and resonant, impossible to square with his coarse manners and loud clothes.

Halfway through the song, a gaggle of girls in identical black strapless sheaths with numbered tags pinned to their waists spilled through the door. Despite the heavy makeup, I could tell they were young, a few maybe even in their teens.

Out, out, the police chief said, waving his arms as if herding cattle.

Only karaoke tonight, said Kaiser Shih.

The girls sheepishly filed back through the door. The vice mayor kept singing without missing a beat.

The police chief exhaled a ring of cigar smoke and rolled his eyes. I already told them when we arrived, No girls.

Kaiser Shih handed me a glass of champagne, which I resolved not to drink, and said, Sorry about that.

I asked, What are the tags for?

He pretended not to understand the question.

The numbers. On the girls.

Oh, that. So you can request the girl you like. But I don't know much about it, I only come to sing.

Is that how Boss Mak and Linlin met?

It was a sincere question, but Kaiser Shih snickered. Linlin has a college degree. She'd die if she heard you.

My headache surged back with a vengeance. I combed through my purse for the Advil bottle, before realizing I'd left it in the hotel room. I thought of the underage factory girls who longed to be waitresses who longed to be hostesses who longed to be mistresses of wealthy old men.

I really don't feel well, I said to Kaiser Shih.

I must have looked deathly because instead of brushing it off, he put down his drink and said he'd call me a car.

The other two men were singing a duet with a swaying salsa beat. They waved and cheerfully told me, Take care, walk slowly, perhaps eager to call the girls back into the room.

Out on the sidewalk, I leaned against a pillar, clutching the orange shopping bag to my chest. When a blue sedan slowed, Kaiser Shih opened the passenger door.

I thanked him and shook his hand.

Until next time, he said.

My chest constricted. I ducked into the car and doubled

over, slashed by the knowledge that I was, irrevocably, one of them now.

What other shady business dealings did these men have their hands in? Horse betting, casinos, perhaps other forms of counterfeits—electronics, pharmaceuticals, worse? Winnie had never voiced any interest in branching out from handbags, but I'd seen how impossible it was to walk away from a profit, how even the firmest moral boundaries could stretch and tear.

LIKE YOU, DETECTIVE, I OFTEN wonder what Winnie's up to these days, whether she's conjured some even more risky and lucrative scheme. And while that would certainly be the most predictable route, I like to imagine she's once again thwarted our expectations, renounced her old ways, and retreated to a quiet beach town to live off her savings. In my fantasy she spends her days cooking, meditating, reading in the sun; she'd take a lover, make new friends. Yes, I know I just mentioned how difficult it is to give up a life of crime, but if anyone could overcome the odds, don't you agree that it's her?

For the last time, Detective, I'm only speculating here. I haven't heard from her since the day she fled. I don't know where she is. I have no clue. Seriously, what will it take to get you to stop asking me that?

PART II

12

When Winnie comes to, she's recumbent in a soft leather recliner, an ice pack draped across the top half of her face. Her eyes throb mildly, as though she accidentally rubbed them after mincing a chili pepper. Her ears fill with the steady soothing rush of waves, the surround-sound speakers so crisp and clear she could be lounging on the shores of a tranquil white sand beach, an icy cocktail and a fat paperback at her fingertips, far, far away from this doctor's office on the thirty-sixth floor of a skyscraper in one of the densest cities in the world.

It had been a colossal headache to wrangle an appointment with Beijing's most coveted plastic surgeon, a man who works only two days a week and whose office wall is covered in signed photographs of him standing beside various Chinese movie starlets, their smooth white faces as indistinguishable as eggs in a crate.

There's a soft knock on the door and the surgeon enters, his low honeyed voice telling Winnie to stay put, relax, don't remove the ice pack. The procedure, he says, has gone exactly as planned. In a few minutes his nurse will be in to explain how to care for the stitches, and then Winnie can be on her way. He'll see her in five days for a routine checkup.

She opens her mouth to thank him, and her voice is a foreign sandpapery hush. If only she could keep it, along with the other alterations.

"Don't mention it," he says and is gone. He's rumored to be so skilled he performs eight double-eyelid surgeries a day.

The anesthetic has yet to wear off completely, and when Winnie lies back, she feels a pleasant rocking sensation, as though aboard an aircraft caught in mild turbulence.

During the initial consultation, the surgeon asked why Winnie was unhappy with her original double-eyelid procedure. She concocted some tale about how she'd had it done in her early twenties, when all she'd cared about was making her eyes appear as large as possible. Now, though, when she looked at pictures of herself, they seemed so unnatural, so fake.

He drew on her eyelids with purple ink to show her different options, saying, "You're right, the trend is toward a more subtle look. The young girls don't want to be cartoons."

His nurse held out a hand mirror and said, "How lovely you are."

Winnie had to hold back a laugh. With her eyes streaked in ink, she resembled a sad clown.

Now the same nurse materializes beside her, helping

her sit up, holding out a little paper cup of water, telling her she can take a look, but not to be alarmed by the swelling and the bruising, all of which is completely normal.

Winnie waves off the warnings and peers at her reflection. Even amid the redness and the puffiness and residual ink stains, it's clear her eye shape has morphed from orb to oval. She turns her head this way and that, admiring the surgeon's handiwork. In a couple of weeks, once she's healed, there'll be appointments for mole removals, lip and cheek injections, eyebrow microblading, hair dyeing. The possibilities for minimally invasive, maximally transformative cosmetic procedures are endless. What a time to be alive. When the cadre of beauty experts is done with her, she'll dare anyone to hold up her wanted notice right by her face and declare them one and the same.

For now, however, she must lie low. She dons a pair of sunglasses with lenses the size of saucers, ties a silk scarf over her hair, and reaches for her orange Birkin. As she walks down the long hallway, the nurse flits around her, insisting she have someone come fetch her, as opposed to making her own way home.

When Winnie emerges into the waiting room, the receptionist joins in, saying, "At least let us call you a cab, Miss Zhou."

Winnie begs them to stop worrying. "It'll take less time to flag one down. I live five minutes away." She's rented an apartment near the clinic, away from the tourists and the major hotels.

Out on the street, the city closes in around her. The autumn chill knifes through her shearling coat and the smog makes her nostrils burn. People speed walk past, clipping her with their sharp-edged briefcases. An impatient driver leans on his horn, prompting others to join in, like a discordant orchestra. After a few shaky steps, Winnie stops to rest and has to admit that the clinic staff's apprehension was not misplaced. Fortunately, a taxi pulls up to let out a passenger and she slides right in.

In her little Dongzhimen rental flat, Winnie double-checks the dead bolt, and then falls back onto the squat hard sofa. All the furniture that came with the apartment is squat and hard, as though designed for ascetic gnomes. On the coffee table, her burner phone springs to life. Momentarily forgetting her condition, she lunges for the retro flip device, and her head swirls, nearly toppling her over. She removes her sunglasses and blinks once, twice to settle her vision. Only one person in the entire world knows how to reach her, but she can't be too careful. She checks the number, sees that it's Ava, and then rejects the call.

WHEN DID SHE FIRST SEE beyond Ava's perfect, unblemished shell to the darkness smoldering within? It must have been back at Stanford, the day Winnie realized she had to leave campus and withdraw from school before the administration figured out what she'd done.

That last afternoon, she'd knelt over her suitcase, hastily

packing her things, as a clueless Ava hovered over her, fretting about Winnie missing her final exams.

"Want me to tell your adviser? I'm sure they'll let you make them up. Kids must have emergencies like this all the time."

Winnie wanted to throw something at her to shut her up. She needed to think. Her Stanford career couldn't be over; there had to be a way out of this mess.

Ava bit her lip. "You know that *Hamlet* essay you've been stressing about?"

Winnie seized a ball of socks and chucked it into her suitcase. Could she please stop talking?

Ava pressed on. "I was thinking you could use mine." (All the freshman humanities courses read *Hamlet* at one point or another.) "I got an A-minus."

Even though the essay had plummeted to the least of her worries, Winnie stopped folding sweaters. She swiveled to face her roommate. "Why would you do that?" If they were discovered — unlikely, but not impossible — Ava, too, could face expulsion.

Ava sat down on her bed and fingered the edge of her comforter. "You would have gotten an A if you'd had time to finish yours."

"But why would you risk getting caught?"

Ava broke into a grin. "I wouldn't get caught. If they asked, obviously I'd tell them you stole it."

And so, a decade later, when Winnie needed reference

letters in support of her green card marriage to Bert, the first person she thought to call was Ava, never mind that they hadn't spoken in ten years.

"Look," Winnie said. "The optics aren't good. He's twice my age. He was married to my late aunt. I need all the help I can get."

"But you do love him, right?" Ava asked.

Winnie fell silent, unsure how to play this, and Ava erupted into laughter. "All right," she said. "I'll do what I can."

The resulting letter was everything the authorities wanted to hear. Ava focused on their time together in college (omitting that it had only lasted a little over two months). She praised Winnie's tenaciousness, her sense of self, her thoroughly American willingness to buck convention and follow her dreams (and her heart!). In less than two pages, Ava framed Winnie's marriage to Bert as nothing short of an act of valor between two kindred souls.

At the start of the interview, the agent glanced at Ava's letter and her face opened up. "My daughter's at Stanford, full scholarship, class of 2012."

This, Winnie thought, was the wondrous paradox of America: they all saw themselves as scrappy outsiders, when in reality they formed one giant country club.

The agent reached across the table and shook Winnie's hand. "Welcome to the US," she said.

Another decade would pass before Winnie reached out to Ava again. This time, she needed to get to her husband, but in the back of her mind she wondered if she might take the opportunity to introduce Ava to a new line of work. (Ava's social media accounts indicated she'd left the firm.) Winnie certainly could use the help, as well as her old friend's tax law expertise.

She only had to hang out with Ava a couple of times before she saw her opening. Of course Ava's Harvard-educated doctor husband was absent and neglectful; of course she couldn't admit that she hated being a lawyer and twisted herself into contortions downplaying her son's developmental issues. As far as Winnie could tell, Ava's entire life could be boiled down to this: great on paper, rotten everywhere else. And Winnie was sorry to see it. Her old friend deserved better. Truly, when Winnie decided to bring Ava into her business, she was doing her a favor. As much as she needed Ava's help, Ava needed hers.

The first step was revealing the counterfeits scheme to test Ava's interest. Winnie convinced Ava to come with her to Neiman Marcus and watch her in action. Afterward, they went to a run-down, deserted coffee shop to debrief.

"But that's cheating," Ava sputtered, once she'd affirmed what she'd seen.

Winnie was prepared. She trotted out her well-worn argument: the corporations were the real villains. They abused their workers, paying them pennies and then going out and hawking the fruits of their labor for thousands. Words she'd spoken so many times, they'd lost all meaning and might as well have been gibberish.

Ava's upper lip curled into a sneer. "Spare me the excuses," she said. "You're no Robin Hood. Just say you saw an opportunity to make money and took it."

Winnie peered down at the greasy table, unsure of how to proceed. "Okay," she said slowly. "You're right. The scheme is foolproof and I'm proud of it. I make good money. Great money, actually, and I could use your help."

When she raised her head, Ava's eyes bored into hers. "You're disgusting," she spat before charging out the door, leaving Winnie behind.

The only other customer in the coffee shop, an elderly man in a fedora, gave a low whistle from behind his newspaper. Winnie sat there, hands clutching opposite elbows, wondering how she'd gotten it so wrong. She'd expected shock, displeasure, sure, maybe condemnation. She hadn't expected rage.

And then she understood: Ava took Winnie's cheating as a personal affront. She saw Winnie as taking something that was rightfully hers—a life of wealth and delight and adventure, a life she'd been promised if only she worked hard enough and followed the rules and never, ever slipped up. Except Ava had done all those things. She'd gone to the right schools, chosen the right career, married the right partner, formed the right family—and made enormous sacrifices in the process, and yet here she was, thoroughly miserable, horrified by the prospect that her entire existence had been built on lies.

In that moment, Winnie was sorry she'd barged back

into her friend's life. She texted an apology and resolved
not to bother Ava again. She even informed Boss Mak that
her connection had fallen through; they'd need to find another way to get his liver.

Who would have predicted that within the week, Ava
would wind up in Hong Kong visiting her family, and that
Oli, that asshole, would freeze her bank cards? That all
these disparate factors would converge to push Ava to take
a peek into Winnie's world and consider it anew?

Once she landed back in San Francisco, Ava called to
report on her Guangzhou escapade. "I can't believe you
sent me into some strange man's apartment." Her voice
was bright. She sounded exhilarated, alive. "I was honestly
prepared to gouge out his eyes with my car keys."

"Please, Ah Seng? He'd probably cower into a shivering
heap the second you threatened him." Winnie wondered if
she should nudge Ava into another assignment or wait for
her to broach the topic herself.

Too casually, Ava said, "You know, Oli offered to give
up his place in Palo Alto."

"But the commute," Winnie deadpanned, and then
dropped the sarcasm. "That's great, though. It's exactly
what you wanted."

On the other end of the line, Ava paused. "I told him to
keep the apartment."

"Why would you do that?"

Ava's voice fell to a mutter. "Like you said, a little independence in a marriage isn't bad."

Winnie's heart was a hummingbird trapped inside her chest. She hadn't expected Ava to commit so quickly to this work.

Softly, almost as though to herself, Ava said, "What kind of husband freezes his wife's bank cards?"

When Winnie didn't answer right away, Ava added, "I know that you know. He told me he ran into you."

Winnie exhaled. "I guess the kind who can't stand not being in control."

"He didn't used to be this way."

This time, Winnie didn't respond because, really, what was there to say?

Now, with Ava fully aboard, the next step was to get her comfortable with returns. Together they drove down to the Stanford Shopping Center to pay a visit to the Chanel boutique. Winnie stationed herself at an outdoor table with a clear line of sight into the store. From behind her oversized sunglasses, she watched Ava glide through the glass doors with the Gabrielle superfake. She nodded at the security guard, the very picture of a woman accustomed to being around people who wanted to offer their help. Casually yet smartly dressed in a loose silk shirt and cigarette pants, her hair pulled back in a low ponytail, Winnie's Evelyne bag slung over one shoulder, Ava exuded money, polish, class, but in a way that had been earned through hard work, not merely granted at birth. That was what made her so likable, endearing. That was what made her the perfect con.

Inside the store, Ava confronted her first decision. She veered away from the Mainland Chinese sales associate to the white one, already a pro. Winnie observed her easy banter, the way she set the superfake on the glass countertop for inspection, and then, right as the sales associate opened the dust bag, held up her own Evelyne as a distraction, pointing out some detail or another. What were they giggling about? What did the sales associate coyly reveal, prompting Ava to graze the woman's forearm as though they were close friends?

It would have been a strong first performance, even without Ava's final flourish—leaving her cell phone on the countertop so that the sales associate would be forced to run after her instead of continuing her inspection of the returned handbag.

Indeed, as the woman pursued Ava out of the store, Winnie noted the way the Chinese sales associate took over her colleague's task, cursorily looking into the dust bag at the superfake without bothering to remove it completely and then toting it into the back room.

"Nice move with the cell phone. How did you come up with that?" Winnie asked when they were in the car, driving back to the city.

"The art of misdirection, right?"

The left-behind cell phone would become Ava's signature move.

Within months, Ava took charge of hiring and training their shoppers. She rented a unit in a nondescript South

San Francisco office park so the shipments wouldn't come to their homes. She incorporated their business in the Cayman Islands and opened them both Swiss bank accounts to maximize privacy and minimize taxes.

Five months into their work together, with profits growing steadily, Mandy Mak called with her preposterous plan to build their own black factory. Ava was the one who pushed Winnie to go along with it.

Following the extended conference call, they locked themselves in Ava's study to go over the details of the proposal.

"Mandy is playing with fire," Winnie whispered, so as not to risk being overheard by Maria, the sharp-eyed nanny. (Ava insisted Maria was safe—the woman was smart enough to know it was better not to know—and while Winnie concurred, she always took extra precautions.)

"It's an audacious move," Ava agreed.

"If any of the brands even suspect what she's up to, Mak International will be done for."

"Thankfully," Ava said, "that's not our problem."

Winnie started. Even after observing the way Ava addressed their shoppers, her ruthless pragmatism still occasionally took her aback.

Ava continued. "Here's how I see it. If we decline to sign the contract, they'll be free to replace us. They'll find some lackey to implement your genius scheme exactly as we've done, and then it's all over for us."

"But if we say yes," said Winnie, "the balance of power

flips completely. They control the inventory. We're at their mercy. We work for them."

Ava sank her fingers into her hair and massaged her scalp, as though that could somehow clear the blockage in her brain. "Unless they're in our debt. Unless they owe us, like really owe us."

Winnie didn't follow. The Maks were so connected, so influential. What did they lack that they couldn't easily procure?

"Like, what if we did them the kind of favor that is impossible to repay? The kind of favor that engenders eternal loyalty and gratitude?"

"Like, say, by giving Boss Mak the liver transplant that saves his life?"

"Or, barring that, leading him to hold out hope that we'll eventually make it happen."

The nape of Winnie's neck tightened. She pictured Boss Mak's cheekbones jutting out of his gaunt, sallow face, his Adam's apple protruding like something that should be kept under wraps.

Ava softened her tone. "Look, I'll do everything I can to convince Oli to do the transplant. But just in case."

In this way it was decided: they would sign the contract rendering the Maks sole supplier of their counterfeit bags, and they would reap the profits that came with it—profits that they would then direct into a new, even more innovative and lucrative scheme. All Winnie had to do was come up with it. For wasn't creativity at the core of her work?

Wasn't it the reason Winnie loved the job? In this business copycats were an occupational hazard, and only the most inventive, the nimblest, deserved to stay on top.

From Dongguan, Ava reported the discussions had gone smoothly. The new factory was even better than they'd hoped. She ticked off Manager Chiang's advancements: instead of a traditional assembly line, workstations were arranged in the shape of a U, with the sewing machines on one side and the assembly on the other, to cut the time it took to pass work from one station to another. Yes, Ava said, every second counted, as evidenced by the plastic signs displaying the precise number of them needed to complete each task.

"You should have seen these workers. So focused, so efficient." It didn't hurt that they were paid nearly as well as their legitimate counterparts, unheard of in black factories.

Ava told Winnie about meeting a young worker, no older than fourteen, who shyly revealed that her salary was enough to put her little sister through school. "Westerners love to talk about ethical labor without asking what the laborers want themselves."

"You tell 'em, sister," Winnie said. Her use of such Americanisms always amused her friend.

For the celebratory dinner, the men had taken Ava to the rooftop restaurant of the Great World Hotel, the cacophony of gaudy glitz that was Boss Mak's preferred spot.

"I've never seen so many bottles of wine for so few people," Ava said. "And all of it ultraexpensive, ultra-French."
Matching the men drink for drink, she felt like she was
back at her old law firm, with limitless youthful energy
to burn.

The accompanying meal had floored her. How long had
Ava spent describing the Peking duck, cooked in a special
oven transported over from Beijing, fueled with freshly cut
wood from apple and date trees that infused the meat with
intense aromatics?

The men treated her like the guest of honor, keeping
her glass full, offering her the choicest morsels, including
the sweet, tender cheeks of the fried grouper.

Winnie had worried that they would consider Ava an
outsider and hold her at arm's length, but her friend assured her they'd gone out of their way to make her feel
welcome.

"They really tried to talk to me, to get to know me.
Thank god Kaiser Shih was there to translate."

This, Winnie always knew, was Ava's superpower—
her ability to make people want to take care of her. She
projected such harmlessness, such innocence, and that rendered her lethal.

After dinner came karaoke in a swanky private room
decked out with an immense TV screen, state-of-the-art
acoustics, psychedelic disco lights, endless whiskey and
champagne.

"You should have seen the men's faces when those

hostesses barged in," Ava said. "They were so embarrassed. It was kind of sweet."

The men chose songs they thought she'd know—by ABBA, Bryan Adams, Madonna, Bon Jovi. Before long they were all on their feet, yelling in unison, shimmying and shaking, clinking their glasses again and again and again.

At some point in the evening, Ava lurched out of the room to stealthily pay the check. On the way back, to tease the men, she peeled off a few bills for the manager and told her to send in the girls. They spilled through the door in their identical black dresses right as the opening notes of "Dancing Queen" filled the room. The men hollered in protest until they saw Ava in the doorway fighting to suppress her laughter. Everyone joined in to sing. The girls draped their thin arms over the men, swaying their hips from side to side. The police chief took Ava by the waist and twirled her around the room, surprisingly agile for someone of his age and girth, while Kaiser Shih rattled a tambourine.

"You can dance, you can jive," they blared into each other's faces, "having the time of your life."

Hours later, ears ringing, throats hoarse, they staggered outside. Was that dawn bleeding into the eastern sky or merely the lights of downtown Dongguan? The men took turns clapping Ava on the back, complimenting her alcohol tolerance, and thanking her for footing the bill. Before she climbed into her ride-share back to the hotel, they hugged one another and slapped palms like teammates who'd won the big game.

Hearing Ava recount all this, Winnie felt an almost parental pride.

THREE WEEKS LATER, MANAGER CHIANG'S first batch of superfakes arrived at their rental unit, ready to be mailed out across the country to their shoppers. The Bottega Veneta Pouches and Dior Book Totes and Valentino Rockstud bags, in all the latest colors and finishes, were so precisely rendered that a one-to-one grading didn't do them justice; these were in a tier of their own. The shoppers returned the bags to unsuspecting boutiques, while their real counterparts flew out of Winnie and Ava's eBay store. Profits doubled, spurred by handbag fanatics on the online forums, who raved about Winnie and Ava's merchandise as well as their customer service.

Where do they get their bags? How do they get them so quickly? How do they stay in business? more than one user asked. I bought my beige-and-black Gabrielle from them at retail when there was a waiting list at Chanel, and other sites were selling lightly used versions at a premium!

To keep up with demand, Ava hired more shoppers and fanned them out to buy, buy, buy. (And return, return, return.) And through it all, Winnie and Ava reminded each other to never get complacent or let down their guard. They communicated with their shoppers via an anonymous Telegram account; they ignored interview requests from nosy fashion bloggers and journalists; they paid a service to scrub the internet of any details that might link their identities to their business.

In the end, though, despite their meticulousness and rigor, all it took was a single innocuous act to send the entire enterprise crashing to the ground.

The instigator was one Mary-Sue Clarke of Canton, Ohio, an otherwise unremarkable woman who happened to have turned fifty in October, three months after Ava signed the new contract with the Maks. To mark the occasion, Mary-Sue's husband, Phil Clarke, gave her a Louis Vuitton Clapton wallet in the iconic Damier canvas. Phil had purchased the wallet at a Neiman Marcus in Orange County while on a business trip.

As Winnie's private investigator would later report, Mary-Sue was thrilled with the gift—that is, until a mere few days later, when one of the tiny golden screws holding together the weighty clasp suddenly loosened and disappeared, rendering the wallet unusable.

To be fair, this was a design flaw on the part of Louis Vuitton and not indicative of the Mak factory's workmanship, not that the distinction would have mattered to Mary-Sue. Dismayed by the quality of this so-called luxury item, she paid a visit to her neighborhood cobbler, who told her it'd be impossible to find a screw that would be a perfect match. She had no choice, then, but to get in her car and drive to the nearest Louis Vuitton boutique, an hour away in Cleveland.

There, a saleswoman with a sharp asymmetrical bob donned a pair of white gloves to examine the wallet—an affectation that Mary-Sue must have found theatrical, pretentious. The woman assured Mary-Sue that the wallet would be sent off to their workshop for repair, which would, of course, be complimentary because Louis Vuitton stood by their goods.

Mary-Sue left satisfied. From the car she phoned her husband to tell him the good news but was interrupted by another incoming call. It was the store manager. In a clipped manner he informed Mary-Sue that further inspection had revealed that the wallet wasn't one of theirs. He used that phrasing exactly.

"What do you mean?" she asked.

"This isn't a Louis Vuitton wallet, madam."

"What are you talking about? It says LV all over it."

"I'm sorry, madam, but it isn't an authentic Louis Vuitton."

"How can that be? It's from Neiman Marcus."

"I suggest you take it up with them."

After more back and forth, the manager told Mary-Sue that store policy technically dictated that they confiscate all inauthentic goods, but if she returned before the end of the day, she could retrieve her wallet.

And so she pulled off the freeway—in rush hour traffic, no less—and went back to the boutique. The young woman who'd been so helpful earlier handed over the wallet pinched between thumb and forefinger, as if it were a dead fish.

Once she was back on the road, Mary-Sue called her husband and berated him. How could he have humiliated her so? Why hadn't he simply told her the truth? What else had he lied about? Would the diamond solitaire on her finger turn out to be cubic zirconia?

Phil Clarke, by nature calm and taciturn, knew to let his wife finish her rant. When she finally paused to take a breath, he said, "It cost one thousand and eighty dollars, plus tax. I kept the receipt in case you wanted to exchange it."

That evening, he and Mary-Sue called the Newport Beach Neiman's. They spoke to a supervisor who apologized profusely and offered an immediate and full refund, plus thirty percent off their next purchase. The supervisor also requested that they mail back the wallet for further investigation.

From there, things would swiftly unravel.

Overnight, Neiman Marcus tightened their policies, subjecting all returns of luxury leather goods to an extra layer of scrutiny. One of Winnie and Ava's most reliable shoppers, a Korean American grad student who used the screen name Purse Addict reported walking into the Boston Neiman's in Copley Square, right before closing time, to return a Balenciaga City superfake in hot pink. She grew wary when the sales associate unzipped the bag's inner pockets and felt around as though looking for a breast lump, and then squinted at Purse Addict's credit card (though the woman was way too young to need reading glasses). Turning her back on Purse Addict, the sales associate got on the phone and called for an "authenticity expert" to come to the floor.

Immediately, the shopper lunged for the replica and slipped out the doors.

A couple days later, another shopper ran into the same problem at a Neiman's in Dallas. This time, the sales associate hung on to her credit card and never gave her a chance to get away. Thankfully the Bottega Veneta woven clutch in question, a particularly excellent replica made from fine intrecciato grosgrain, passed muster, and the return was accepted. But the shopper was so shaken she resigned minutes later.

Soon, it was clear that their Asian and Asian American workers were being racially profiled. What had once been their greatest strength—their perceived docility and obedience, their relative invisibility—had become their weakness. The narrative flipped. Now their Asian features read as scheming, perfidious, sly. Word spread from Neiman's to Saks and Nordstrom and the rest. All the department stores unleashed stricter return policies. Profits plunged. The Maks demanded to be paid for inventory, even if the superfakes were simply piling up in their South San Francisco office unit, their car trunks, their homes.

Once law enforcement got involved, Winnie and Ava studied their predicament from every angle before concluding they had no choice: the handbag scheme had become a liability, and, like a gangrenous foot, they had to saw it off to survive.

But even if they shut everything down before the most incriminating information was uncovered, it was too late to clear their names.

Sitting before her laptop in her Los Angeles penthouse, Winnie purchased a ticket on the last flight out of LAX and then called Ava. "There's a midnight flight from SFO to Taipei with one seat in business class."

"You can't be serious," Ava said. "I can't just pack up and go."

Winnie looked out the floor-to-ceiling windows of her bedroom. How she would miss this sky, so clean and blue, with clouds so fluffy they appeared painted on. She said, "I'm going to spell this out for you. We are a step away from being arrested and thrown into prison for months, maybe years. I'm getting the hell out of here, and I strongly suggest you join me."

"And what do you advise I do with my son?"

"Is Maria there?"

"Winnie, don't be absurd."

Winnie jumped up and paced the room. "It's temporary. We can figure out the details later."

"You want me to leave my kid behind indefinitely?"

Winnie turned and kicked the wall, stubbing her big toe. "What do you think will happen when you get locked up?"

Her words were met with silence on the other end.

"Ava?" said Winnie. "Ava, did I lose you?"

"I'm here," she said, her voice eerily composed.

"There's no other way, you hear me?" Winnie drummed

her fingers on her dresser, trying to figure out how to make her friend understand. "There's no other way."

"Wait," Ava said. "I think there might be."

Winnie pressed her forehead into the palm of her hand. They didn't have time for this.

"What if, instead of waiting for them to arrest me, I turn myself in?"

Winnie bit down on her thumb to hold back a shriek. "Then you'll go to jail for sure."

There again was that same self-possessed tone. "Not if we execute this exactly right."

IN BEIJING, THE SUN HAS begun to set. Its rays slice through the blinds, striping the floor like the bars of a cell. The stiff couch cushions make the muscles in Winnie's lower back ache. She rolls onto her side, trying and failing to get comfortable, wondering why the pain seems to have spread to her head. She checks the clock on the mantel. Of course. It's time for her meds. She places two pain tablets on her tongue and goes to the bathroom to gulp down water. Bringing her face close enough to fog the mirror, she squirts a layer of thick translucent ointment onto her mottled, puffy lids, tender as an infant's skin. To her reflection, the only soul she's spoken to, really spoken to, face-to-face this entire month, she says, "Here's to new beginnings."

She carries her laptop to the bedroom, flips down the quilt, and climbs into bed without changing her clothes. Opening the computer, she pulls up the video she's watched at least once a day for the past week. The video is produced by a major British newspaper. It features a diamond lab in Cardiff, Wales—yes, a lab that grows diamonds that are apparently indistinguishable from natural stones, though a good deal cheaper, which is, of course, where the opportunity lies. For why not take the counterfeit handbag blueprint that worked so well, and shift it fifteen, thirty, forty-five degrees? This time, though, they'll supervise the entire supply chain from beginning to end. This time, they will not cede control.

Again she watches the scientist place the tiny diamond seed into the complicated-looking growth chamber; again she watches the seed grow in minuscule increments within a cloud of purple light. In a few weeks, the scientist says, this seed will be a full-blown diamond, ready to be cut and polished and set in a ring. Winnie imagines weighing the rough stone in the palm of her hand, and her heart thuds like a kettledrum. She hasn't told Ava yet, not until she has a clearer picture of what the plan will entail. Besides, Ava doesn't need any distractions right now.

On the nightstand, Winnie's burner phone clatters against the wood surface. She checks the number and this time she answers. "Well? How did it go with the detective today?"

"So far, so good," Ava says evenly.

"And what am I supposed to do with that?"

"What did you say about getting too confident?" Ava reminds her. "It's going as planned, but there's a long way to go."

"At least tell me what you said."

Ava dives into the events of the previous day, the way she regaled the detective with stories of heartbreak and alienation—her dying marriage, her repulsion toward Winnie and those menacing men.

"Listen to this," Ava says, her voice rising in pitch.

Winnie can see her now, eyes blazing, cheeks flushed, unable to contain her excitement.

"I told her the factory girl was missing two fingers, and, Winnie, you should have seen her face."

Winnie screams and then covers her mouth, shaken by the sound her own body produced. How did Ava come up with that? Her friend could have been a bestselling novelist, effortlessly spinning tall tales from golden thread. What will she invent next? A gangster with a raised scar spanning temple to jaw? A sex worker who dreams of going back to school? Winnie can't wait to find out.

13

You know, Detective, that moment in a story when the main character realizes she's made a commitment she can't rescind and going forward seems the only available option? What's it called—the point of no return. Well, that's how I felt at the end of my trip to Dongguan. Out of options. All I could do was put one foot in front of the other, complete the minimum required to satisfy Winnie and the Maks. I thought I could cordon off my work and maintain that barrier, quarantine it in another dimension to prevent it from contaminating my real life and the lives of the people I loved.

But I could not control my dreams. Back at the hotel after that surreal and debauched evening, I crumpled into bed, only to be plagued by nightmares of fingerless children bearing tin cups of poisoned water. I awoke to the sun beating down on me, coating my skin in a suffocating sheen of sweat. My stomach churned, my calves and arches ached, and yet I was determined not to spend another second in this sordid town. I had to get across the border to Hong

Kong to see my grandmother and the rest of my family, to remind myself who I really was.

I understand, Detective, that the timing of my grandmother's birthday might seem coincidental, and I don't know what more I can say to convince you otherwise. She was born on July 17, 1930. There's nothing made up about that. Yes, her ninetieth. Ah, I see the confusion. Ninety is her Chinese age, not her Western age. Chinese people believe babies are born at the age of one because they count the months spent in the womb.

No, I can assure you I had no other reason to go to Hong Kong. From my hotel in Dongguan—you can see right here, I checked out at 10:02 a.m.—I went straight to the restaurant, ate lunch with my family, got back in the car, and went to the airport for my evening flight. No detours, no stops.

And I'm so grateful I went. Not only because I was there to celebrate my grandmother, but also because she is part of the reason I sit here before you now, telling you everything I know about Winnie, her associates, and this whole despicable affair.

What does my grandmother have to do with anything? Well, Detective, picture me showing up at the famous dim sum restaurant in Causeway Bay. It's Saturday at noon and the light-filled room bustles with large multigenerational families just like mine. All around me children shriek with joy, and parents scold, and grandparents cluck indulgently. You could not imagine a more wholesome scene.

Over there at a prime table by the window is my family: My grandmother in a new floral blouse with freshly washed hair. My aunt and uncle who have taken charge of the ordering. My cousin Kayla; her husband, Winston; and their two little girls, all clad in lucky red to mark the occasion. My other cousin Karina has even flown in from Singapore with her boyfriend, Hugh, a tall, slouched Australian dressed in head-to-toe athleisure.

In that moment, I fingered the crimson silk scarf knotted around my throat and was restored to myself. These were my people, these clean, cheerful, bright-eyed souls, not those sleazy da kuan from the night before, dripping in dirty money.

At the sight of my cousin's round-cheeked daughters, ages six and four, a hole yawned open in my chest and I longed to squeeze my goofy little boy. The girls were called Dana and Ella and they were stunningly well-behaved, conversing easily with the adults, downing dumplings with gusto.

When the little one, Ella, had eaten her fill, she climbed right into my lap to tell me, first in Cantonese and then, when it was clear I was having trouble following, in English, about the new kitten her father had brought home.

I asked its name.

He's called Bear.

My cousin Kayla caught my eye and beamed.

I said, What an interesting name.

The little girl pushed the back of her head into my sternum and chortled up at me, the sound so pure and clear

that in that moment, I was sure she was an angel, an other-
worldly sprite. The previous twenty-four hours sloughed
off me like flakes of dead skin. This, I reminded myself, was
real. This was the true me. I was a mother, an aunt, a wife. I
was a woman who was loved. I was the opposite of Winnie,
with her severe, solitary life.

I told Ella that her cousin Henri would love to play
with her kitten the next time he was in Hong Kong, and
she gave me a look of disbelief. A cousin? she cried. Who
I don't even know? Who I've never met in my entire life?

Karina's boyfriend reached over and pinched the girl's
little nose and said, You silly thing, before asking what I'd
been doing in Dongguan.

It seemed as though the entire table quieted to hear my
answer. Oh, boring stuff. This and that, I said.

What kind of boring stuff? Karina asked.

I reached for my cup and took a long sip of tea. I'm
working for a friend's consulting business—she connects
American brands with Chinese manufacturers. I was relieved when my cousin's eyes glazed over. But how about
you? Do you like living in Singapore?

Karina told me about her first day in the city, how she
watched a woman toss a cigarette butt onto the ground
outside a shopping mall, and instantly a plainclothes cop
materialized—where had he been hiding?—to cite her for
littering.

Hugh added, It's a beautiful spotless place, but at
what cost?

I sat back and listened, thankful to be out of the spotlight, to have this time with my relatives, listening to their lighthearted workaday stories.

No, in all seriousness, Karina said, as much as I love Hong Kong, it's gotten way too difficult to practice medicine here. She explained that at her old position she'd been expected to work across the border at the Shenzhen clinic half the week, where more and more, the rich Mainland Chinese seemed to believe money could buy the perfect medical outcome. The stress had aggravated her gastric ulcers. Her hair had fallen out in clumps.

Aunt Lydia said, We miss her, but we're glad she moved.

Uncle Mark said, Last year a doctor was stabbed to death by a patient who complained he felt worse after surgery—at the most prestigious hospital in Beijing! That's just one of several assaults on medical workers.

I nodded solemnly, arranged my features into a look of deep concern, but in my mind, I was picturing the men from last night, calmly extracting demand after demand. More than a gift or an extravagant bribe, that crocodile Birkin was a warning, a threat. It sat beside my luggage in the trunk of that Mercedes in some overpriced parking garage nearby. If only someone would break into the car and take it, so I'd never have to see it again. If only someone would break into my life and abduct this version of me that Winnie had created, so I would never have to be her again.

My grandmother interrupted my thoughts. Ava, you look so tired, so skinny. You're working too much.

It's jet lag, I said.

Do you have someone to take care of you at home?

I couldn't recall ever being asked this question so frankly, and suddenly I wanted to cry. Sure, I said. I have Oli. I have friends. The answer sounded feeble even to me.

Friends, my grandma said, are not the same.

I smiled weakly. Where was she going with this?

I'm ninety years old, my friends are dead!

I'm your friend, Hugh said inanely.

My grandma patted Hugh's sleeve and retrained her focus on me. She said, I used to worry so much about your mom in America. I worried she wouldn't have people around when she was old. You and your brother lived so far away. With a trembling hand, she dabbed her napkin to the corners of her eyes.

My ears filled with a phantom roar. Please don't worry about me, Popo, I said. I'm fine, absolutely fine. Here, I'll eat another egg tart to gain some weight.

What wouldn't I have given to buy my mom another month, another week, to have her beside me at this table with her mother, her sister, the rest of our family? I wanted to learn more about my cousins, to give Henri the chance to get to know Dana and Ella. The thought of wasting one more day at the mercy of Winnie and her associates sickened me.

En route to the Shenzhen airport, I pictured the life my mom might have led if my dad had forgone graduate school in Massachusetts and they'd remained in Hong Kong—the weekly family meals, her loved ones a subway ride away. I thought about my dad, all alone in that big rambling house he refused to leave. I thought about my brother, who'd recently suggested we both fly to Boston for the anniversary of Mom's death, to which I'd replied that work was too busy, and I couldn't take another trip. I thought about Henri, my precious, impossible boy, and how he had even less family than I had, our shrinking lineage an upside-down triangle balanced precariously on its tip.

When he grew old, when we were gone, who would he confide in? Who would give him advice? Who would save him from making the same senseless decisions his mother had made?

For a while I studied the back of my driver's head. Say, I said, were you born in Shenzhen?

Oh no, he said, no one's actually from here.

Weaving deftly through traffic, he told me it took twelve hours by train to reach the countryside to see his family. He went every year during the Spring Festival, when the trains were so packed that if he were to let go of his bag, it would be held in place by all the passengers crammed in beside him.

Are your parents sad that you're so far away?

He stopped at a red light. Probably a little.

A mass of pedestrians flooded the crosswalk, clutching purses and shopping bags and the hands of small children.

I said, You must get homesick from time to time.

Never, he said, thumping his chest, I'm a city boy now.

And do you like this job?

He glanced back at me and grinned. I won't be a driver forever. I want to run my own business, a whole fleet of cars and drivers, chauffeuring businessmen around town.

At the airport, he pulled up to Departures, put the car in park, and ran around to remove my luggage from the trunk. I thanked him and wished him good luck with his career plans.

See you, bye, he said in English.

I fought the impulse to throw my arms around this young man and tell him to take care of himself, to work hard and not be swayed by all the dirty cash flowing through this city, for there was no shame in good, honest work.

But who on earth was I to be doling out such advice? Instead, I said simply, See you, bye.

FROM YOUR PERSPECTIVE, DETECTIVE, I can see how this all sounds. Why did it take me three more months to turn myself in and come clean? Believe me: if I only had myself to worry about, I would have sped to your office the instant my plane touched down in San Francisco. But I am selfish; I am weak. I feared for my husband, my son, my beloved ninety-year-old grandmother, who was only a border away from those heinous men. For that, I am sorry. I am sorry I thought I could somehow extricate myself from Winnie's grip. I'm sorry I thought I could protect my family from them. Most of all, I'm sorry I didn't grasp right away that the only thing that would save us was the truth, nothing but the truth.

14

I arrived at the door to my home, ready to make amends to my husband, to do everything in my power to shield him from my mistakes. As far as I could tell, there was only one way to guarantee his safety: I would have to convince him to take Boss Mak on as a patient, while ensuring he knew nothing about the man's criminal background.

I'd spotted a crystal vase at Duty Free that was a reasonable replacement for our shattered Baccarat, and now I held out my offering to Oli and said, I'm sorry.

Stretched out on the sofa, he lifted his head an inch and then flopped back down as though overcome by the effort that minor action had demanded. What's that?

A vase, I said. I set the shopping bag on the carpet.

His eyes had that glassy catatonic look he'd sometimes get after one of those brutal forty-eight-hour shifts that are now considered too sadistic for residents.

What happened? I asked. What's wrong?

Henri scampered over wearing nothing but a diaper, though a chill gusted through the open window. I held out my arms for a hug, but he peeled off and made for the remote control on the coffee table, which he then bashed against a couch cushion in a failed attempt to turn on the television.

Oli remained immobile, his face contorted in agony.

What happened? I asked again. I leaned over and kissed the top of my son's head, which smelled like yeast and wet dog, and not at all of shampoo. He craned back, flashing the most beatific smile, and returned to bashing the remote.

Oli stretched his arms overhead and let out a monstrous groan that startled Henri, who mimicked his papa and giggled at his own joke. I scooped up my son and kissed both his cheeks, and he squirmed out of my embrace.

At last Oli said, I tried to potty train him.

Oh no.

I wanted it to be a surprise.

Oh no.

I didn't think it'd be that hard. They said one to three days.

A bolt of annoyance shot through me, obliterating my good intentions. It was so typical of my husband to take on challenges no sane person would ever attempt. He was never more energized, more motivated than after being told something simply could not be done. It's how he completed a double major in physics and biology at Harvard, while rowing on the novice crew team and serving as backup accompanist with the dance department. It's how he survived surgery residency and fellowship. It's how he was named a UCSF Rising Star his first year as an attending. And then it came to me: it was also how I might get him to operate on Boss Mak—by framing his new patient as the pinnacle of his career, one that he alone could crest.

I leaned over and sniffed Henri's diaper. It smelled clean.

Obviously, I gave up, Oli said, flinging the back of his hand over his eyes, as though to hide his shame.

What happened?

He pooped on the carpet.

Oh no. I scanned the beige rug until I spotted the tell-tale whitish patch of cleaning fluid beside the coffee table. The blue plastic potty seat we'd ordered weeks ago was pushed up against one wall, next to the *Everyone Poops* book and Elmo doll.

And then he pooped on the bathroom floor, right by the toilet, to make a point.

Henri!

My son regarded me, all eyelashes and pink cheeks, and then resumed his quest to turn on the television.

And I'm not even getting into all the times he peed.

I went to the sofa and squeezed in next to my husband. He rolled onto his side to make room.

I'm so sorry, I said.

He draped his arm across my chest. I cannot remember ever bombing so miserably at anything.

Frustrated with his inability to decipher the remote

control, Henri pressed his face to the TV screen and released a shrill whine.

Oli moaned, Turn it on, please, for the love of god.

I put on *Thomas the Tank Engine*. Henri was immediately
quiet, swaying to the beat of the theme song, ignoring my
command to not stand so close to the screen.

When I turned around to raise the topic of Boss Mak,
Oli was already snoring. Another of my husband's salient
traits is his ability to fall asleep near instantaneously, regardless of whether he's in a crowded call room or a five-star
hotel.

While Henri drooled in front of the television, messages
from Winnie streamed in on my phone.

> How is the factory setup? How many bags come off the
> line each day? What new styles are we expecting? How
> many shoppers do we need to hire?

The only way to slow her down was to answer her
questions one by one. If I put her off, it would lead to esca-
lation, and the last thing I wanted was her calling my home
phone, or worse, showing up at my door if she was in town.
And no, Detective, I didn't bother telling her about the dis-
turbing scenes I'd witnessed at the factory. By then I knew
there was no point; all she'd do was scoff at my naivete, the
same way Kaiser Shih had.

I was studying the season's most important designer

look books, debating Winnie over what the biggest hits would be via text message, when in my peripheral vision, I saw Henri trip over his own feet and topple into the TV stand.

Dropping my phone, I lunged at him and checked for blood as he howled in rage.

I know it hurts, but you're okay. You're okay, Cookie.

Still prone on the couch, Oli said groggily, You let him watch cartoons for two whole hours? What were you doing this entire time?

All at once, I saw how dense I'd been to think for even a moment that I could keep this work out of my home; I'd already failed. And so I spun around and took out my anger on Oli.

Who asked you to potty train him? Why the hell did you think that would work?

Confused and groggy, Oli contemplated me. I wanted to do something nice for you.

Henri howled louder to get our attention.

You weren't helping, I said. You were showing off.

Oli sat up on his elbows. What are you talking about?

Next time you want to help, come home from work at a decent hour and put your son to bed.

He recoiled as though he'd been slapped. I waited for him to fight back—after all, he'd spent the whole weekend with Henri on his own. Instead, he bent over and scooped up his son.

Viens, mon petit, he mumbled into Henri's hair, t'inquiète.

Together they left the room, leaving me to confront my own ugliness and despair.

LATER, OLI AND I MOVED around the bedroom like a couple of roommates who'd only recently met.

Excuse me, he said, reaching across me for his toothbrush.

Do you mind? I asked when I pulled more of the comforter onto my side.

We lay as far apart from each other as possible on the king-size bed. He turned off the bedside lamp, and I knew that despite our residual resentment, there was a good chance he'd fall asleep at once. I could no longer put this off. I had to ask him about the transplant.

Okay, I'm sorry I snapped, I said, aware of how much apologizing I'd been doing lately.

He responded with a grunt.

Thank you for taking care of him while I was gone. You're a good dad. And even though I meant every word, I felt manipulative, cheap.

He turned to face me. In the dark I could make out his strong, symmetrical eyebrows, his straight high nose.

All right, he said. Apology accepted.

I scooted closer to him, planting my head on the broad plane of his chest. Have you made a decision about Boss Mak?

Actually, yes — after reviewing his test results and scans, I can't recommend him to the committee.

I launched myself upright using Oli's chest as a spring-

board. He yelped in pain. I hadn't expected such a defini-
tive answer.

I think you should reconsider, I said.

He sat up too. The man has every comorbidity in the
book—high blood pressure, prediabetes, heart disease.
He's a terrible candidate. An unrepentant alcoholic. And
he's old.

He's not that old, I said. He's the same age as my mom.

Seventy is old.

My head was a tangled skein of emotions. You need to
understand, Detective, first and foremost, I had to appease
Boss Mak. But at the same time, a part of me genuinely
empathized with him. For wasn't he a father and a husband
and a beloved boss? Didn't he have people who depended
on him, just like me, or my mom, whom I hadn't had the
chance to save?

He'll stop drinking, I said, though I knew it seemed far-
fetched. And he's offered that huge donation.

Oli said, I've told you this before. We don't have enough
livers as it is. The vast majority of patients die waiting in
line. I can't in good conscience give a liver to some rich
foreigner.

I pointed out that one liver wouldn't alter supply in a
substantial way, and, furthermore, Boss Mak's donation
would be instrumental in providing services for patients
who couldn't afford to pay for them.

He snapped on the lamp and squinted at me. Why do
you care so much? You barely know this man.

I forced myself to hold Oli's gaze. He wants to be treated by the best, and that's you. He'll have Development earmark that five-hundred-grand donation solely for your use. You can finally expand the free-housing program like you've always wanted.

Oli looked up at the ceiling and seemed to consider my arguments. I reminded him that, yes, Boss Mak could easily find another hospital to take his money, but what would they invest it in? Cutting-edge research that would benefit only the tiny percentage who received transplants? Another overpaid endowed chair? Fancy artwork and light fixtures?

He shook his head, exasperated. The stuff that does the most good—housing assistance, nutrition assistance—is always the least sexy and therefore the least funded.

Exactly! I said.

All right, he said. I'll think about it. I'll see what I can do.

He turned out the light and pulled me into his arms. In the dark I clung to him, riding the ebb and flow of his breath. Within seconds he was fast asleep.

WAS I SURPRISED BY OLI'S willingness to skirt medical guidelines? First off, Detective, I'm not sure that's how I'd characterize his actions. These judgments about whom to treat are complicated and nuanced. I'm no expert, so I can't give you details about how Oli and the committee eventually decided to accept Boss Mak as a patient. You've spoken to Oli—didn't you ask him yourself? Oh, right, of course, medical confidentiality. Then, I suppose, we'll never know for sure.

Besides, why does any of this matter when the transplant's never going to happen? Ah, I see, you still suspect Oli knows more than he claims. But I can assure you he told you the truth. How could he have known about Boss Mak's criminal activities when he knew nothing about his own wife's? Yes, I do mean absolutely nothing. As you've already observed, my marriage around this time was, well, strained. When Oli and I weren't fretting over Henri, we essentially led separate lives. Quite frankly, it's a miracle we're still together, and I thank the universe for that every day.

Listen, my husband is highly ethical, the most moral person I know after my mom. But he's no mindless follower of the rules. It would be a mistake to conflate the two. It takes courage and creativity to live a principled life.

You know that ethical dilemma about the trolley barreling down the railway tracks? No? Okay, so there's a runaway trolley heading straight for five people, who are tied up and unable to move, and you're standing some distance away in the train yard, next to a lever that can divert the trolley to another set of tracks, but then you notice there's a single person on those other tracks. What do you do?

You probably won't be surprised to know that most people would do nothing—that is, they'd let the trolley kill those five people—and then tell themselves, later, that the situation was out of their control. Only the truly brave and good take action and divert the trolley. They kill one to save four. That's Oli. He never opts for the easy way out. He chooses action. He takes a stand.

One last thing: I don't know if you've been informed that Oli was just promoted to chief of surgery. We received the news last week. Why would Stanford promote someone they didn't trust or believe in one hundred percent? Clearly, they agree Oli had zero knowledge of Boss Mak's background. Hopefully, in this new role, he'll be able to direct more funding to the free-housing program, even without Boss Mak's donation. What more can I say? He's a good man. We're all so desperately proud of him.

15

It's true, Detective, about a month after my trip to Dong-guan, I flew to Boston, with Henri in tow, to see my dad. I already know your next question, and the answer is no, absolutely not. I did not mention one word about what I'd gotten myself into with Winnie—not to my dad, nor my brother, nor my sister-in-law.

I know this is hard for you to believe, but Asian families are different from white families. We don't talk the way you all do. I mean, we talk, of course we talk, but not about our fears, our pain, our deepest, darkest secrets.

When I was little, I envied the kids whose parents served us wine coolers at parties and offered to drive us home. You know, the if-you're-going-to-drink-I'd-rather-you-do-it-with-us type. My parents were the opposite: If you're going to drink, don't. And if you persist, don't you dare let me find out. I remember Carla telling me freshman year that over winter break her mom had taken her to the doctor to get birth control pills, and being filled with sheer wonder.

Did I wish my parents were more like theirs? More *American*, so to speak? Of course I did. Who wouldn't? It's something I thought about the entire time I was home, as I vetted and hired six new shoppers to keep up with our growing inventory and worried the more we expanded, the greater our chances of being felled—all while insisting to my family that everything was fine, just fine, better than fine.

I'd come home because my dad had finally agreed to put the house on the market and move into a condo in Chicago, not far from where my brother and sister-in-law lived. He needed help packing, and, given that it had been over a year since I'd last seen him, I could not say no. My first night there, once Dad and I had wrestled Henri into bed, we retreated to the back porch with cold bottles of beer. It was the end of August and scorching hot. Above our heads the ceiling fan churned, and I lifted my face to the breeze.

Dad started in with, Have you taken him to a specialist?

My cheeks burned. I pressed the bottle to my skin. Please, Dad, not now.

Okay, no need to get worked up, he said.

My phone vibrated in my pocket, and I reached down and silenced it. I'd asked Winnie to please only text if it was urgent, but already, in the five hours I'd been home, Dad had commented on my copious phone use.

He took a swig of beer and ran his thumb over the label. Anyway, like I told Mom, Henri doesn't have to be a genius. It's more important that he's a good person. Honest, kind.

Really? You said that? Can I get it in writing? I asked. I didn't have to remind my dad that my grades were the only thing he'd harped on when I was growing up.

It was his turn to bristle. That's because you were good at school. We were encouraging your natural gifts.

And look at what all those A's and A-pluses got me, I said.

What's that supposed to mean?

I pointed out that being a corporate lawyer was the kind of job one tolerated, endured.

He scowled. I never wanted you to worry about money. At least your law degree got you that.

I gazed into the amber depths of my beer bottle. You don't have to hate your job to make money.

Sure, and you don't have to love it either. It's called work.

All at once, Detective, the bushel of lies I'd lugged everywhere for the past seven months bore down upon my shoulders, threatening to crush me. In my desperation, I forgot who I was and how I was raised. I blurted, I can't do this anymore.

I lifted my gaze, both terrified and brimming with hope.

Dad's eyes grew big. He reared back his head and inhaled sharply before he managed to seize control and flatten his features once again. He asked mildly, What do you mean?

Already he'd retreated beyond some invisible barrier, like a dog behind a wireless fence.

And what had I expected? This had always been our way.

Oh, nothing. Henri's at such a difficult age is all.

Dad's entire face relaxed. He won't be two forever.

Thank god for that.

We drained our bottles. The moment passed.

And I'm so glad I restrained myself in time because now, from where I sit today, confessing everything to you, I see what I couldn't as a child: to share one's secrets is to force others to bear your burden; to stay silent is to spare them.

I REALIZE I HAVEN'T SAID too much about my brother, Gabe, but perhaps it'd be helpful for you to know a little about him, to understand my upbringing and how I became the emotionally thwarted person who spent nearly a year under Winnie's spell.

In many ways Gabe and I are opposites, and because of that I shouldered my parents' hopes while he floated above the fray. My brother was popular in school, outgoing, a star athlete—regionally ranked in tennis as a junior. He didn't work too hard in class, earned mostly B's, got into a small liberal arts college in Connecticut. Upon graduation one of his frat brothers helped him get a job selling medical devices. He ended up being really, really good at it. He's a managing director now. Also, a stellar golfer.

And to this day, my dad has never acknowledged Gabe's

success. He views his son as this relaxed, carefree guy who happens into situations and somehow comes out on top. My mom used to say that Gabe was more lucky than gifted — yes, to his face, that's the Asian way. But you don't get one promotion after another without working for it, even if it's (as Dad would put it) only sales.

Once when I was in middle school, my dad berated me for getting a B-plus on a math midterm, and I shouted, Why don't you ever get on Gabe?

It was the first time I'd ever talked back to him and he shot my mom a dark look before spitting out, Because he isn't as smart as you, his tone making it clear this wasn't a compliment.

Gabe must have been at tennis practice, but I scoured the room to make sure.

Dad softened his tone. Everyone has different talents. Yours is school. Don't waste it.

The adrenaline rush from standing up to him made me combative. I said, It's not like you yell at Gabe when he loses a match.

Tennis? Dad said, his voice dripping scorn. Tennis is a game, a hobby. Your brother is no Michael Chang, all right? He'll be lucky to play D-3.

This scathing, clear-eyed assessment shut me up. For the rest of the semester, I worked my butt off to make up for that B-plus, and, in the end, I got my dad his A.

What's that, Detective? Yes, the phrasing of that struck

me, too. *I got my dad his A.* But that's how I've always felt—like I was living my life for someone else. First my parents, then Oli, and now Winnie. In fact, I was so used to moving on autopilot toward some externally defined goal that I never stopped to consider where I wanted to go in the first place.

Look, I'm thirty-seven years old and, I'm sure we can all agree, way past being able to credibly blame my parents for who I am today. But that, I think, is the point. I'd never really grown up. I was still that nerdy teenager who dared not dream her own dreams, who craved approval from whoever would offer it.

GIVEN DAD'S DIM VIEW OF Gabe, you may be wondering how he ended up moving to Chicago to live near his son. The decision astounded me, too; I hadn't realized the sale of the house was up for discussion—nor how much I'd missed in the time I'd been working for Winnie.

Long story short, Dad's decision was the result of a monthslong campaign waged by Gabe and his wife, Priya. Once they'd discovered that Dad's chronic knee and hip pains—the result of decades of road running—had intensified, forcing him to give up his daily walks, they decided to take action. Priya found a nice new condo building two L stops away from their town house, next to a gym with a pool Dad could use instead of pounding down the sidewalk. She seeded their conversations with only slightly embellished descriptions of the amenities, making sure to include how much she and my brother wanted my dad to be around to speak Mandarin to soon-to-be-born Ajay and his future siblings, while also promising that they would never coerce him into babysitting. When Gabe and Priya flew out to see Dad on the anniversary of Mom's death, they made a final push, brandishing evidence from Gabe's Realtor friend that demonstrated the unit was a good buy and would definitely appreciate in value.

Hearing all this filled me with guilt, yes, but also envy. My warm, plucky sister-in-law had started calling my parents Mom and Dad the day Gabe proposed. Oli, on the other hand, had grumbled when I'd informed him, shortly after the funeral, that I'd hired my dad a housekeeper and planned to pay for it, too.

And Dad said yes? I asked Gabe over the phone. Just like that?

My brother paused. I mean, it took months to convince him, but, yeah, eventually, he said yes.

I'm sorry I've been so busy, I said.

Yeah, yeah, he said. Ava's working, nothing new.

You've done so much for Dad since Mom died. I'm sorry I haven't helped.

Looking back, I hear the plea in my voice. Ask me, I'm saying. Ask me why I'm working so much. Ask me what I'm doing. Ask me what's wrong.

Thank god he didn't.

No worries, Gabe said. There's plenty of time for you to take a turn.

As I've already shown, Detective, skirting conflict is the Wong family religion.

THE FOLLOWING DAY, AN EMAIL from a fashion journalist appeared in my personal account. She'd come across our eBay store and was so impressed by the inventory that she wanted to interview me. I didn't know how she'd tracked me down, given that I'd paid a service to scrub all personal information off the internet. I deleted the message without responding and checked the online forums.

Overnight, it seemed, our eBay store had risen in prominence, spurred by handbag fanatics who raved about our Bottega Veneta Pouches and Dior Book Totes and Valentino Rockstud bags. The forums teemed with questions about how we managed to procure the latest styles so quickly. Users speculated that our store traded in factory overruns or even stolen goods. (By the way, Detective, overruns are a myth. As I've already mentioned, the brands demand that every millimeter of raw material be accounted for—no factory is running off ten extra bags without Saint Laurent immediately figuring it out.)

A text from Winnie arrived, crowing about yet another style that had sold out. I wanted to hurl my phone on the ground. Why couldn't she see the problem bubbling beneath the surface? She'd built this business on anonymity; this was way too much publicity, too much buzz.

In the midst of all this, my brother and sister-in-law arrived from Chicago—Priya, thirty-six weeks pregnant and glowing; Gabe, tanned and smiling beneath a Roger Federer baseball cap.

My brother and I spent the afternoon packing things in boxes and trying to convince Dad to sit in front of the television and rest his creaky joints. Meanwhile Priya and Henri dug holes in the backyard with old spatulas, since the new owners were going to tear up the lawn anyway.

How's Oli? Gabe asked. Still working like a maniac?

Always and forever.

The question would have annoyed Oli. Why is that the only thing your brother ever asks? he'd say, to which I'd explain that Gabe didn't really know what his job entailed (and didn't really care). Oli found Gabe and Priya conventional and unambitious, *basic*. But I didn't see it that way. To me, their most striking quality was their utter contentment with what they had. They weren't strivers, and it seemed a wonderful way to be.

After we'd packed up the last of the study, Gabe and I stood by the window, watching Priya and Henri traipse around the backyard in search of treasure.

How much maternity leave does she get? I asked.

Three months, and she's taking it all and quitting right after.

No! I said.

Yes!

Down below, Priya and Henri settled on a pair of gardening stools and filled a yellow pail with dirt.

Good for her. She earned that leave. I couldn't help

adding, But maybe she shouldn't burn all those bridges. In case she ever needs a reference.

Gabe playfully flicked my forehead, which infuriated me as much now as it had when I was a kid. I flicked him on the cheekbone, and he twisted my arm behind my back.

Ow, I said.

He laughed and let go. Thanks for the advice, nerd, but she's never going back. Her lifelong goal is to be a stay-at-home mom.

Priya called Henri's attention to a butterfly flitting around the bushes, and he squealed and gave chase, flapping his spatula about his head.

They really are best buds, said Gabe.

I didn't answer, distracted by the chiming of my phone. I reached into my pocket. Another email from that same journalist, informing me that if I didn't agree to talk to her, she would go ahead and write the article outing me anyway. This time I forwarded the email to Winnie with the subject heading: PROBLEM!!!

What are you working on that's so urgent? Gabe asked. You haven't stopped checking your phone.

From the next room my dad called, Kids, get in here. You have to see this.

We looked at each other and went to the den. Mouth agape, Dad pointed at the TV screen, where a downed airplane smoldered on a runway.

You must remember this crash, Detective, the one at

SFO. The plane was carrying seventy Shanghainese students who'd enrolled in a San Francisco summer camp to learn English, as well as five of their teachers. At the time, I had yet to discover the role that counterfeit plane parts had played in the crash, but I recalled those da kuan sitting around the table, boasting about sending their kids to pricey camps like this one, in between oblique references to their other illegal dealings.

Together my dad, my brother, and I watched that plane land just short of the runway, striking the seawall, severing its tail as cleanly as a hot knife through butter.

According to the CNN reporter, two high school girls, best friends, had been ejected from their seats—their seat belts hadn't been fastened. They died almost instantly. A shot of the school hosting the summer camp filled the screen. It was the one on Noe and Twenty-Fifth, blocks away from my house. How many times had I passed the colorful welcome banner shrouding the gate?

The longer I sat in front of the television, the more convinced I was that this story was personal, that it somehow belonged to me. Maybe it's because this was every mom's worst nightmare. Or maybe it's more abstract than that— I'd gained a window into China and the way the whole country barreled ahead at breakneck pace, ignoring the cracks, and something about that ethos told me this plane had not crashed by chance.

When my brother suggested changing the channel, I voiced my dissent, unable to look away from the parents

gathered in some nondescript Shanghai meeting hall, waiting to hear what had become of their children. All across
the room, couples collapsed into each other's arms, whether
from grief or relief, it was impossible to tell.

But I apologize, Detective, this is getting off topic. I
think we've covered the essentials about my visit home.

What's that? You have my brother on record saying
I told him about my work selling counterfeits? In the car
when we went to pick up dinner?

No, that's a complete misunderstanding. He didn't
mean it that way. It's true I tried one last time to tell him,
but he didn't believe me. The whole thing sounded so out-
landish he took it as a joke.

Let me explain. The same day we learned of the plane
crash, Gabe and I went to pick up a couple of pizzas for
dinner. We were in Dad's car when another message from
Winnie made my phone buzz.

Don't worry, she wrote. I'll take care of it.

I knew that she'd already sent her private investigator
to dig up dirt on the journalist—anything that would coerce her into abandoning the article. I pictured a tenacious
young woman, a year or two out of journalism school, hungry, eager, making barely minimum wage.

When Gabe asked who was on the phone, I was too
weary to lie.

Winnie, I said. Remember her?

Winnie who?

Winnie my freshman roommate.

The one who cheated on her SATs?

That's the one.

You're still in touch?

I told him I worked for her now.

Oh yeah? Doing what?

I watched my brother check his blind spot before switching lanes. He still drove with only one hand, torso leaned all the way back in his seat, the very picture of a man who was pleasantly surprised by how well his life had turned out. And right then, Detective, I longed for even an ounce of his security, his ease.

Heart battering my chest, I said, Importing counterfeit designer handbags.

His head jerked toward me.

My vocal cords spasmed but I continued. It's a whole scheme where we return fakes to department stores and sell the real bags on eBay.

I felt my facial muscles contort into a gruesome rictus, an effort to interpret the conflicting signals of relief and terror lighting up my brain.

My brother's eyes bugged out, his forehead creased, and then he exploded with laughter. Good one, good one, he said. You're a regular Bonnie and Clyde.

You got it, I said.

When he'd calmed down, he asked, What do you really do?

Contracts for her handbag manufacturing business. Boring stuff.

He turned into a strip mall and parked in front of the liquor store he'd frequented as an underage teen. I fumbled with the seat belt buckle. My fingers felt stiff and sore, as though stricken by arthritis.

Oh god, remember this place? he said, already moving on. Remember when Mom found that six-pack under my bed?

So, you see, Detective. Even though, yes, technically I confessed my crime to Gabe, there's no way he absorbed what I'd said. In fact, I'm certain that he wouldn't have recalled that part of our exchange if you hadn't probed him.

Now if my mom, not Gabe, had been in the driver's seat that day, then perhaps things would have unfolded differently.

What did you just say? she'd ask, deadly slow, after I'd spat out my confession.

Unable to backtrack, I would race through the whole repugnant story while she listened, first uncomprehendingly, and then gradually growing enraged.

Did this so-called friend of yours hold a knife to your neck and threaten to kill you if you didn't comply? she'd demand. No? Then you weren't forced. You chose to do it. You wretched girl, you stupid child. I've always had a bad feeling about that Winnie.

I would let my mother's words pummel me; I'd submit to every one of her blows. And in that moment, despite her anger and disappointment, I'd no longer be alone.

I'll take you to the police myself, she'd say, and my whole body would release.

Turn yourself in and face the consequences.

I know it took a bit longer than it should have, Detective, but I did finally listen to her, and I'm here now. What else can I tell you? What more do you need to know?

16

Four days after her double-eyelid procedure, Winnie unlocks the front door to the sound of her burner phone ringing in the bedroom. She turns the dead bolt and hurries toward it, shedding her sunglasses. The number that flashes on the screen is local, one she doesn't recognize. She rejects the call before remembering the only other person besides Ava who has this number — the marketing and PR strategist she's hired to do some preliminary work for the new diamond venture. He's done a day early; she's not surprised. Here in China, no task is ever deemed impossible, no demand too extreme, no deadline too tight. There's always someone younger, scrappier, hungrier, willing to work harder, faster, longer. Need a high-speed rail station in nine hours? Or a 1,300-ton bridge in a day and half? Not a problem. Done and done.

It's one of the reasons she's hiding out in Beijing, despite Ava's initial incredulity.

"You've got to be kidding," Ava said during that last conversation before Winnie boarded her flight out of LAX. "Anywhere but there."

Winnie argued that her homeland checked all the boxes: no extradition treaty with the US, no chance of the Chinese police cooperating with their American counterparts. In Beijing, Winnie is far enough away from Dongguan to hide from the Maks, yet close enough to keep tabs on them. Because it's imperative that the Maks believe their business is thriving, that all is well. The entire plan hinges on Boss Mak boarding a plane in three hours and arriving in San Francisco for his medical appointment—the only person important enough to give up in Winnie's place, the key to securing a lighter sentence for Ava.

Indeed, all this time, as Ava's submitted to Detective Georgia Murphy's questioning, she's maintained communications with the team in Dongguan, paying for inventory with Homeland Security funds—inventory that goes straight to the department to be used as evidence in the case against Boss Mak. To explain Winnie's absence, Ava told Mandy that she's flown off to a silent meditation retreat in the Arizona desert. It will buy them another day, which—assuming his flight leaves on schedule—is all they need.

Winnie applies another coat of ointment to her eyelids before checking the clock. Boss Mak should be about ready to head to the airport. She sees him standing in the circular driveway of his mansion, instructing the driver to load the matching set of Rimowa luggage into the Range Rover. Perhaps Mandy has left work early to see her father off. (Mandy's mother, who remains Boss Mak's wife only in name, certainly won't bother emerging from her wing of the house.)

"The next time we see each other, you'll be a new man," Mandy might say.

Boss Mak would scoff. "I'm the same old guy regardless of the age of my liver."

"So does that mean you won't come into work to micromanage me, no matter how good you feel?"

"I promise nothing," says Boss Mak. "As long as I'm alive, Mak International will always be my company, and you will always be my baby girl."

Father and daughter embrace.

Winnie's eyes sting. She plops down on the bed and stuffs her hands beneath her seat, waiting for the urge to pick up the phone and call him to subside. Nothing will happen, she reminds herself, for the next fourteen-plus hours, until the flight touches down in San Francisco. To help pass the time, she goes through her routine of checking Mandy Mak's social media pages. In addition to being a businesswoman, Mandy is a socialite and fashion icon with tens of thousands of followers. Several times a day, she documents her designer outfits, her fancy restaurant meals, her adorable Scottish terrier, Butterscotch.

This afternoon, her photos of a cappuccino adorned with an intricate milk-foam rose and a pair of sapphire satin Manolo Blahnik mules strike Winnie as strangely melancholy, shot through with longing, though, of course, this is ridiculous. There's no way Mandy has a clue of what's to come.

In addition to the photos, there's a new video clip, filmed at a gala a week earlier thrown by one of those high-society glossies that's featured Mandy and her lavish town house multiple times. Mandy's dressed in a bubblegum-pink halter-neck ball gown with a plunging neckline. "It's Armani," she says, giving the camera a flirtatious wink. "I was inspired by Gwyneth Paltrow at the Oscars. Remember? Back when she won for *Shakespeare in Love?*"

Winnie's about to close the clip when a face in the corner of the frame catches her eye. The person interviewing Mandy from behind the camera notices too.

"Is that your father?" the interviewer asks. "Did he come with you?"

"Dad," Mandy calls, reaching out and tugging on the sleeve of his jacket, as the interviewer blathers on about the most stylish father-daughter pair in town.

Boss Mak lurches into the frame, and Winnie feels her throat constrict. Purple shadows ring his eyes, giving his face a ghoulish cast. Even thinner than before, he looks like a child trying on his father's tuxedo. As he makes his way over, he lists to one side, and Winnie spots the cane supporting his weight. The clip ends before he has a chance to speak.

Winnie shuts her laptop and pushes it away, as though that could somehow erase the image that has already wormed its way deep into her skull.

ALL EVENING, WINNIE IS TOO tense to eat anything, to do much more than watch the clock. Now Boss Mak is taking his first-class seat; he's wiping his face with a steaming-hot towel in between sips of champagne; he's flipping through *Duty Free* magazine; at last, his plane takes off.

After a fitful night's sleep, Winnie leaps out of bed at dawn and turns on the television to CCTV.

At first, it's business as usual: afternoon showers in the forecast, traffic on the Jingha expressway. What follows is a lively segment on China's first food court powered by artificial intelligence. Despite herself, Winnie studies the robotic arms that deftly dunk wontons into bubbling oil. She watches a customer place a bowl of seafood noodles on a smart cashier desk that instantly calculates the cost of the meal. The pride that rises within her quickly gives way to skepticism when she spies a weary worker in the corner with a rag in hand, ready to clean up the robots' spills. What is the point of all this? Another case of tech for tech's sake.

CCTV disagrees.

"What an achievement!" Dee Liu, one of the morning news anchors, exclaims.

Her coanchor jokes, "How do I get one of those installed in my kitchen? My wife could use the help."

All at once, the mood in the studio shifts. Dee Liu touches her earpiece, listens intently, and apologizes for interrupting her coanchor. Speaking straight into the camera, she says, "Breaking news—we've received reports that businessman Mak Yiu Fai, head of handbag manufacturing giant Mak International, has been arrested at the San Francisco International Airport."

A grainy video, clearly filmed on a cell phone by an unsteady hand, fills the screen. Winnie turns up the volume. In the video, an old man in a wheelchair is rolled out of the boarding gate and into the terminal. Despite Boss Mak's wizened form, his navy sports coat looks freshly pressed. Flanking him is an attractive young woman in a cashmere sweat suit, whom Dee Liu identifies as his personal assistant, but who Winnie knows is his mistress, Bo Linlin.

Whatever Boss Mak says to Linlin draws her eyes away from her phone. In a flash they're surrounded by a team of law enforcement agents.

"You're under arrest," one of them says, handcuffing Boss Mak's child-size wrists.

He protests in Mandarin. "What are you doing? This is preposterous. Linlin, tell them we have a medical appointment at Stanford. Tell them Dr. Desjardins is expecting us."

An agent handcuffs Linlin, too, and she starts to cry.

"Stop it," Boss Mak urges. "Tell them, tell them!"

The young woman opens her mouth but only wails emerge.

Winnie's stomach plunges. She shuts her eyes. On-screen, Boss Mak continues to bark orders at Linlin, full of vigor to the last.

"Who's that old dude?" the amateur videographer asks as the pair is led away. "A drug dealer? A mob boss?" He drops the phone and curses. The video ends.

All morning CCTV replays the clip on a loop, interspersed with incensed commentary from the anchors. How dare the Americans arrest a helpless grandfather who was only seeking medical care. How dare they allow this upstanding businessman to pledge a five-hundred-thousand-dollar donation to one of their elite hospitals and then turn him in to law enforcement. How dare they disrespect an entire nation.

After a while, Winnie mutes the newscasters, though she remains glued to the screen.

They won't send him to prison, Ava's told her, not in his condition. He'll receive all necessary medical aid, even if his dreams of a new liver have vaporized. Winnie knows these words are meant to comfort her, but the last thing she wants is to ease her guilt. She made the choice to trade his life for hers; at the very least, she owes it to him to feel every ounce of remorse deep within her bones.

Now she asks herself the question she's posed so many times before: Could there have been another way? A way that didn't involve betraying the man who helped change her life. Should she have pushed harder for Ava to flee with her? Would it have been so intolerable to be stranded in China for the rest of their days? To never walk freely in America again?

As usual, the last question is the one that does her in. "I'm sorry," she says aloud, as though her words could somehow reach Boss Mak. And she is, truly sorry, from the bottom of her heart, but the answer to that question is yes. What was it he used to tell her? "Everyone has a price. The trick is figuring out what it is without overpaying." Well, she's unearthed America's price for her freedom, and that price, not a penny more, nor less, is him.

Her laptop chimes, informing her of a new email. It's from the hardworking marketing strategist who must have grown impatient waiting for her to return his call. Dazed and queasy, she reaches for the remote and turns off the TV, glad to have something else to do. She clicks on the link to the new website for her fictional family-owned jewelry business, Hopkinton Jewels. The business is based in Hopkinton, New Hampshire, USA (pop. 5,589), a place she landed on after poring over photographs of New England's famous fall colors. Soon, once their social media pages are up and running, she will visit Beijing's premier diamond labs, seeking out the perfect partner for their next venture.

She still hasn't told Ava about these developments, not yet, not when they're so close. There'll be plenty of time to catch her up once all this is over.

17

How does it feel, Detective, to finally arrest the man you've been tracking all these months? You likely have a better understanding of the breadth of his criminal activities than I do, now that it's clear that counterfeit handbags are only one small part of his empire.

You took him into custody before he had a chance to pressure Winnie and me to participate in his other ventures, but trust me when I say it would have happened eventually. Our competitors, for instance, had begun streamlining their operations, packing bags of fentanyl pills into their counterfeit purses to save on shipping costs. And if Boss Mak had wanted to implement this, Winnie and I would have had little recourse. As I've already said—and as I'd warned Winnie months earlier—they controlled the inventory; we had no choice but to submit to their orders.

So I can say unequivocally that the Maks and Winnie and I were not a team. He was the boss, and we were his employees, or, perhaps more accurately, he was the kingpin, and we were the pawns.

Case in point: when the department stores tightened their return policies last month, and our shoppers went into a panic, and counterfeits piled up on our shelves, do you think the Maks told us to take our time, assess the situation, and come up with a solution? No, they demanded to be paid on schedule, regardless of whether we could put those handbags to use. Does that seem like the attitude of a business partner to you?

At the same time, Detective, I don't want you to think I gave up Boss Mak as an act of revenge. This is first and foremost about taking responsibility for my actions. Believe me when I say that I would have found my way to you, whether or not you'd found your way to us.

So why did I wait until November 1 to give myself up? That's a very good question. Because I knew you could arrest me on the spot, and I had to be sure that my son would have someone to take care of him. He's only three. Sorry, I'm sorry, I never cry. I'm embarrassed, this is so unlike me.

THAT'S KIND OF YOU TO offer, but I don't need a break. I want to keep going. You see, back in September, Maria had decamped for a British expat family in Laurel Heights once Henri started preschool, leaving us without a nanny. Two and a half weeks later, he proceeded to get himself kicked out. (Yes, almost exactly when the department stores caught on to us.)

How did he get expelled, you ask? Well, by crying non-stop for seventeen days straight. And lest you think I'm exaggerating, I can assure you I was there to witness it all. Adhering to school policy, on each and every one of those days, I'd accompany my son to the classroom, plant him in his seat, and tell him I'd return in fifteen minutes. Then I'd wait in the teachers' lounge for the specified amount of time, come back to check on him, and tell him I'd return in thirty minutes, and then forty-five minutes, and so on and so forth. So I can say for certain that Henri never stopped crying. His stamina was frankly impressive. He'd sit in his chair in the back corner of the room, red-faced and wailing, while the other children sang and danced and played and listened to stories.

On day seventeen, when Principal Florence Lin invited me into her office, nestled her chin in the basket of her hands, and said, He's young to begin with, keep him at home for another year, all I could do was slump in my chair, exhausted to the point of delirium.

What choice did I have? I took him home and tried to convince Maria to come back. But no matter how much money I offered, she gently but firmly refused. So here I was in the house, alone with my kid, trying to meet Winnie's demand to figure out a way to get around the department stores' new policies, while simultaneously soothing our spooked shoppers, all in the couple of hours in the afternoon that the new babysitter dropped in to plant Henri in front of the iPad and talk to her sister on the phone, as though I wouldn't notice.

As a mother yourself, you must see where I'm coming

from. I couldn't risk getting myself arrested and stranding my son with this indifferent community college student for who knows how long while his father toiled away in Palo Alto. I needed a better plan. I wasn't foolish enough to think I'd find another Maria, but maybe someone who wasn't simply in my home to collect a paycheck, someone who actually cared about Henri.

MEANWHILE, WINNIE WAS FORMULATING HER counterattack against the department stores.

I got it, she said. We'll hire a white shopper.

I was clearing the lunch dishes while listening to yet another potential nanny read to Henri in the other room. What are you talking about?

If Purse Addict and the others are right that they're being racially profiled, then we have to adapt. We hire white people.

Focused on extricating myself from this job, I said, All right. Whatever you say.

And that, Detective Georgia Murphy, is what led Winnie to hire you.

Now, perhaps you might fill in a couple of blanks for me. Am I right to deduce that you'd been monitoring our eBay store for some time? That we'd attracted attention by putting out limited editions earlier and earlier, so much so that the brands had begun to take notice? That's what I feared from the start.

From what I can gather, you purchased one of our bags

on eBay—a Mansur Gavriel bucket bag in camel (excellent choice, by the way)—took it to a professional authenticator, and determined it to be the real thing. This raised questions about how we could be turning a profit, since all our bags were listed at, or even slightly below, retail price.

A search for reviews of our store led you to an online forum for handbag fanatics who raved about our merchandise. Digging into different topics on the forum, you came across a thread of disgruntled Neiman's shoppers who claimed to have been sold knockoffs, which led you to a Reddit community of die-hard replica buyers, which led you to Winnie's job posting. Have I got it right so far?

As you saw for yourself, Winnie took pains to make the posting look like a generic want ad for secret shoppers, the kind hired by legitimate companies to pose as buyers to help them evaluate their customer experience. It's only after an applicant had been vetted and hired that Winnie provided further information about our business—and always via an anonymous Telegram account.

On a hunch you posed as an ordinary suburban mom who happened to love high-end replicas and was looking to make some extra cash. Like I said, Winnie was desperate. She hired you at once. She started you off with a basic assignment. You were to go to Bloomingdale's, pick up a Longchamp Le Pliage in mustard, and ship it to our P.O. box. You swiftly completed the task, prompting her to send the corresponding superfake to your address.

I'm guessing you needed the replica in hand to obtain

the search warrant that allowed you to eventually uncover Winnie's identity? Of course, back in October, neither Winnie nor I had any inkling you were onto us. We were too busy managing the inventory that was piling up on our shelves—handbags that I turned in to your team, every single one in our possession.

Naturally, like you, I noticed the discrepancy in numbers. My records show there should have been an additional two hundred units. I can only assume that Winnie managed to liquidate those bags sometime at the end of October before fleeing the country. She certainly needed the cash.

You're saying that Boss Mak confirmed as much? He told you a contact informed him that those two hundred superfakes changed hands on October 26? Of course I'm stunned. How would he know that? Who would have told him? But if you've verified the information and believe it to be true, then you must be right. Winnie wasn't in the Bay Area then, but I suppose she could have easily sent a lackey to our office unit in South San Francisco to get the bags and make the sale. By this time, she strongly doubted my commitment and had accused me multiple times of slacking off, so it makes sense that she'd manage the liquidation on her own.

I hope you're not suggesting that I sold those bags and stashed away the funds. That would have been impossible. You see, Detective, October 26 was the day of my fifteen-year college reunion. You have my cell phone location data;

you can see for yourself that I was down in the Peninsula all day, despite my reluctance to be there.

Why didn't I want to go? Imagine the situation, Detective: Here I was, at what had to be the very nadir of my life, forced to confront the most accomplished people on the planet. I felt like the brunt of the universe's sick joke, the laughingstock of Silicon Valley, the punching bag of the global elite.

Carla and Joanne must have sensed my anguish, because that morning, I awoke to a flurry of text messages, warning me to not even think about backing out.

Carla typed, I'll even pick you up. Door-to-door service. I won't take no for an answer.

In the end, my friends agreed to let me skip the official on-campus events in exchange for coming to our classmate Aimee Cho's backyard brunch.

As Carla already told you, she picked me up at around 10:30 in the morning and drove me straight to Aimee's Woodside mansion, where I remained until approximately 2:30 in the afternoon, at which point I hitched a ride back to the city with another classmate, Troy Howard. At no point in the day did I go to South San Francisco—not to offload our inventory nor for any other reason.

What can I tell you about the party? It was one of those perfect Northern Californian fall days: a crisp seventy degrees, a cloudless blue sky, all that overflowing golden light—the kind of day that only seemed to underscore my miserable mood. Gripping my elbow, Carla pulled me into the group taking a tour of Aimee's newly redecorated home. As my friends swooned over the sustainably grown Brazilian teak floors and the dining room chairs upholstered in mint Thai silk, I tried to figure out how to convince Winnie to stop hiring shoppers, white or any other race, to pause all operations until we had answers. Her primary objection would obviously be the loss of revenue, but that was paltry compared to getting caught.

Again and again I answered my classmates brightly, I'm focused on my son right now. I'll start looking in earnest once he goes to preschool. Oh, we decided to wait a year because he only just turned three.

That's so brave of you to take a break, Aimee cooed. She was a fellow dissatisfied corporate lawyer.

Her husband, Brent, who did something in finance that earned him ten times her already ample salary, added, Aimee was sending emails, like, fifteen minutes after delivering.

She mimed slapping him across the face; he pretended to strangle her. They laughed and pecked each other's cheek. Everyone else laughed along, and I followed suit, a split second behind, like an alien desperate to appear human.

Let me be clear, Detective. It's no exaggeration to say that at this moment in time I was failing on all fronts: as an employee, a wife, a mother, a friend—hell, as a flipping Stanford grad. What I wanted more than anything was to crawl into a cave and hide from my shortcomings, the polar opposite of what I'd walked into.

Retreating to the bar, I asked a uniformed bartender for a mojito. When Joanne spotted me and waved me over, I downed as much of my drink as I could before joining her. She was with Javier Delgado, who did something important at Google, and Javier's partner, Andrew.

We donate a hundred bucks to the alumni fund every year, Joanne said, pointing out her son, who dashed past squealing in pursuit of a pack of children (all of them, no doubt, potty trained and enrolled in school). It's a small investment in the future.

We need to get on that, Javier said, smacking his partner's elbow.

Andrew rolled his eyes and stage-whispered, We're not even sure we're having kids. He turned politely to me. Do you have kids?

What's that? I said, struggling to keep up with the conversation.

He repeated the question.

Oh, yes, one.

Her husband works at Stanford so they don't have to donate, Joanne said.

Say, said Javier, is anyone in touch with Winnie Fang? I heard she's back in town.

Joanne looked at me.

A little bit, I said. She comes to SF for work from time to time. I didn't elaborate.

Predictably, the conversation turned to the SAT scandal of our past, and to how it compared to the more recent

Hollywood scandal, and then to another classmate who'd been arrested for insider trading, but had successfully fought the charges with the aid of a costly lawyer, and was back at a hedge fund and richer than ever.

I chugged the last of my drink and went to get a refill, ignoring Joanne's raised eyebrows.

I assume, Detective, that Joanne told you she lost track of me for, say, half an hour midway through the party? That's because Winnie called while I was waiting for my drink, and I had to dart into a bathroom to talk to her.

We have to pause all activities, I said. Just until we figure out what's going on. We can't risk a shopper getting caught.

Wrong answer, Winnie said. I asked for solutions, not this.

How can I solve a problem we don't fully comprehend?

With that kind of attitude, you'll never come up with anything good.

Around and around we went, talking past each other, unable to reach a compromise. At last, she ended the call, and I turned on the tap to assuage the suspicions of anyone waiting outside. (That's how paranoid Winnie had made me.) Rinsing my hands, I observed my reflection in the mirror, the deep groove between my eyebrows, the luster-less eyes and pinched mouth. Who was this craven person looking back at me, expecting to be told what to do?

Outside, I paused by the patio doors, taking in this backyard abounding with power brokers, all tanned and relaxed, basking in their success and good fortune, in their lives of plenty and ease. This was what I had lost. No, this was what Winnie had stolen from me.

Soon, my classmates began to head to campus for the football game and various panels and lectures, more eating and drinking. This is when I rode back to the city with Troy Howard and his wife, Kathy. He'd been the sixteenth employee at Twitter and was now basically retired. All the way to San Francisco, they regaled me with stories about their family's travels to Tanzania, Jaipur, the Azores.

Now, of course, we're grounded for a while because the girls are in school, Troy said.

Kathy asked, Where's your little one in school?

We decided to wait a year, I said. Henri only just turned three.

That's good, no rush, Troy said, as though he hadn't mentioned that his girls had been learning Mandarin since birth from their live-in Chinese nanny to ensure truly native accents.

It's worse when parents force things, said Kathy. A friend of hers who'd started her daughter at Ming Liang Academy—you know, the Chinese immersion school?— had told her an absolute horror story about a little boy who'd cried nonstop for weeks and wet himself daily before finally getting expelled.

My mojito-filled stomach churned, sending acid up my gullet, along with the protest that Henri had only wet himself a handful of times. I choked out, How awful.

Troy said, Poor little guy. Who knows how long he'll carry that trauma?

The parents should have known better, said Kathy.

Weakly, I agreed.

When the car stopped at a red light, I briefly entertained the thought of flinging open the door and leaping out, running away from it all, and if I broke a limb or got a concussion, maybe Winnie would finally leave me alone.

They dropped me off in front of my house. Instead of going right inside, I checked to make sure that neither Oli nor Henri had spotted me through a window and jogged up the street, away from them.

When the backs of my ballet flats chafed my heels, I settled on a bench near the bus stop and checked my phone, torturing myself with images of joyous classmates frolicking on our joyous campus, reveling in each other's joyous company. Scrolling through my feed, I spotted a *60 Minutes* clip about the SFO plane crash. The headline declared that counterfeit airplane parts may have been at fault. I pressed play and turned up the volume.

Apparently, Boeing routinely outsourced their manufacturing to subcontractors in China, who in turn outsourced work to sub-subcontractors, who commonly used substandard raw materials and fabricated production records to fool the inspectors.

What's more, Lesley Stahl said, her piercing blue eyes locking with mine, many of those components are what are known as single-point-of-failure parts, meaning if they fail, the whole system fails. Could this have been the culprit of the tragic SFO crash? Investigators are working around the clock to uncover the answer.

My mind landed on the Maks' other illegal businesses. Tell me, Detective, you must have an idea. What else do they manufacture? Counterfeit pharmaceuticals? Electronics? Do you know for certain that the Maks deal in counterfeit plane parts, too? I suspected as much.

Indeed, as I sat on that bench, thinking about those two little girls who'd been ejected from their seats, the lies that Winnie had fed me and that I in turn accepted — that ours was a victimless crime, that we helped more people than we hurt — all of that curdled into a foul, bitter brew.

This, Detective, is the moment I decided I would confess everything I knew about the Maks, Winnie, and, most of all, myself.

Why the skepticism? I've been completely forthright with you; I've laid myself bare.

What's that? You looked up Winnie's green card application file? I have no idea how she could have submitted a reference letter written by me. We weren't in touch back then, so I certainly didn't write it. As I've already said, I didn't even know she'd married and divorced that uncle of hers until Carla and Joanne told me about it. Winnie must have written the letter herself and forged my signature. By now you know as well as I: she'd sign anybody's name with a flourish, if it would help her get her way.

Come on, Detective. You can't still be asking this question, not after everything we've covered. How can I make this any clearer? I do not know where she is.

Why would you go through the trouble of acquiring the call logs for my other phone? Why not simply ask me? Aren't I here, of my own accord, telling you every last detail I know? Haven't I given up every email exchanged with Mandy Mak and Kaiser Shih to substantiate what I've said?

Of course I made some calls to Beijing—and, as you've no doubt observed, Guangzhou, Dongguan, Shenzhen, Shanghai. Up until yesterday, the Maks believed that Winnie and I were running a thriving counterfeit handbag business, and they had absolutely nothing to worry about. How else do you think you arrested your guy?

I'm sorry, I'm sorry, I don't mean to be rude. Let me say, Detective, that it's such a relief to tell you everything. What I want most is to excise this small stretch of time like a tumor, go home to my husband and child, and start anew. What a fool I was to take my beautiful life for granted.

Yes, yes, I know you're not done with me yet. There's more to get through. Where was I? The decline, the fall, the finale.

AT THIS POINT, DETECTIVE, THE story shifts back to you—how you infiltrated our business to build a case against us. Honestly you worked so quickly and efficiently, you likely could have ambushed Winnie at home in L.A. if you hadn't decided you needed additional evidence and asked to complete a higher value assignment.

This is when Winnie grew suspicious. She dispatched her private investigator to dig into your background, and once she figured out who you were, she called to say that at long last she agreed with me—it was time to shut things down.

She said, There's a midnight flight from SFO to Taipei with one seat in business class.

I'm not going, I said.

You must.

I won't.

It was the kind of exchange we'd fallen into countless times these past months. And yet, she must have heard in my voice a new steeliness, a diamond core.

Have you lost your mind? There's no way they won't come after you.

I know.

Her tone dripped acid. Don't think you can bring me down with you. And with that, she ended the call and disappeared.

The phone plunged from my trembling grip. My limbs gave way and I fell to the floor, shaking, sweating, dispelling a fiery animal stink. I was hollowed out, empty, exorcised, reborn. The ground rose up to cradle me. There on the rug I remained for who knows how long, until Henri wandered in, threw himself on top of me, and growled like a lion, thinking it a game.

❊

HOURS LATER, WHEN OLI CAME home, I was waiting for him in the living room. I asked him to sit down on the sofa next to me.

He said, What's going on? Where's Henri?

He's in the high chair with the iPad. He's fine.

Oli kicked off his shoes and joined me, his messenger bag still slung across his torso.

I need to tell you something, I said. I need you to not say a word until I'm done.

He ran his fingers through his hair and said, All right.

Then and there, I told him everything from start to finish. No more secrets, no more lies.

He listened and did not interrupt, his expression growing more and more strained with the effort to remain silent.

When I finally stopped, he said, Now can I speak?

I nodded. My mouth was parched, my throat tender and sore.

When will you go to the police?

First thing tomorrow.

He rubbed the stubble on his chin.

In a small voice I said, Is there anything else you want to ask me?

No, he said gruffly. Yes.

I wet my chapped lips with my tongue.

I still—I just—I—. He couldn't complete the thought.

I stared out the window at the darkening street, and he did, too, anticipating that magic moment when the street-lights glimmered on.

SO THIS IS IT. THIS is everything. I guess the only other thing I want you to know is that I've given a lot of thought to the future and how I will atone for my mistakes. I've started researching MBA programs—I know, can you imagine? At my age? If I'm fortunate enough to go back to school, my dream is to build a direct-to-consumer clothing company that sells luxe basics, produced in the most ethical factories—factories that will provide good jobs for women in the developing world.

I hope to have the chance to be a better mom to my son. This upheaval has been so challenging for him, needless to say, but I'm ready, finally, to be there for him, to focus on his needs and not the things I desire for him. As for Oli, he's still processing what I've told him; of course that'll take time. But the fact that he listened, really listened, and that he's still here—well, that gives me hope. I've started look-ing for a house in Palo Alto. Henri and I will move the instant we're able. All I want is for the three of us to be a family. It's the only thing I've ever wanted. I was a fool to let Winnie convince me otherwise.

Okay, now that's truly everything. I think you'll agree I've held up my end of the bargain, and please, Detective, I'm pleading with you to hold up yours.

18

Three days after her father's arrest, Mandy Mak breaks her silence and gives a televised press conference. Winnie notes that she's traded her high-fashion wardrobe for a muted dark blouse, a thin strand of pearls. When she reads her prepared statement, trembling hands belie her steady voice.

"My father has done nothing wrong. Not only have the Americans locked up an innocent man, but they have also deprived him of lifesaving medical care. In the days to come, I look forward to proving that he's been framed by his former business associates, Ava Wong and"—here, she lowers the sheet of paper and seems to stare right through the screen into Winnie's living room—"Fang Wenyi, who is still at large. People of China, I appeal to you for your help. If you have any information on Fang Wenyi and her whereabouts, please, I beg you, come forward and help this daughter clear her father's name. Justice must be done." Mandy dabs a handkerchief to her eyes and is escorted off the podium.

Winnie has to admit it's not a bad strategy—training

the spotlight on The Americans. Mandy knows the press will seize on Winnie's change of citizenship to portray her as a defector, a turncoat, a traitor to China. Mandy's already shut down the black factory, given up a few rogue employees who were ostensibly in cahoots with The Americans.

Now Winnie finds herself face-to-face with her own image, plastered across the TV screen. The headshot is from her old employee ID card at a German multinational company, her first job out of college. Some enterprising intern must have tracked it down. The photo was snapped before even her first double-eyelid procedure; she reminds herself that she looks nothing like that now.

Turning off the TV, she moves on to the microblogging platforms, where netizens are engaged in fierce debate.

> Every time I see a picture of Boss Mak in that wheelchair I feel sad. He's in his 70s. He deserves peace!

> What are the international brands so angry about? If they want Western-style IP protections, then they should pay for Western labor!

> That Ava Wong and Fang Wenyi are really ruthless, trading in an old grandpa for their own freedom. I stand with Mandy Mak!

Seeing her and Ava's names right there, side by side, makes Winnie reel. She's underestimated Mandy Mak's social media prowess and reach. She longs to lower the blinds and barricade the door, to stay hidden in this apartment until Ava's sentencing next week. At least then she'll know whether she has a future in America, away from this hostile, unforgiving place.

But she's not here in Beijing on an extended vacation. There's work to be done—diamond labs to visit, scientists to consult, sales teams to convince. The few times she has to leave the house, she takes every precaution, using the pseudonym Zhou Feifei, wrapping a silk scarf around her head and donning her enormous sunglasses, even at twilight. (She stops going out at night.)

Returning home from another unsuccessful meeting, during which the diamond manufacturer's sales manager informed her they simply couldn't work with a business as small as hers, she spots a beat-up Nissan parked across the street from her apartment complex. A bald, hulking man sits in the driver's seat. Thirty minutes later, when she slips out to the grocery store, car and driver remain in the same spot. He's smoking a cigarette out the open window, and when she walks past, the cigarette butt dives at her foot, nearly singeing her toes.

She jumps back. "Watch it."

"Excuse me," he says. "I didn't see you there."

Later she tries to explain to Ava why his words seemed so menacing.

"Nobody but me has any idea where you are," Ava says. "And you have to get off Weibo. Those people only know what state propaganda tells them, which is to say nothing at all."

It's the night before Ava's sentencing hearing. She and Winnie have been on the phone for hours, replaying the entire confession from start to finish, trying to discern where they stand. As far as they can tell, Ava nailed the trickiest part of the confession—convincing Georgia Murphy that she couldn't have offloaded those two hundred bags, not while she was at Aimee Cho's reunion party, surrounded by classmates at all times, even when driving back and forth from the city.

Winnie says, "So no one noticed you went missing for almost an hour?"

"I told her I was locked in the bathroom arguing with you!" says Ava. "There were so many people around, Joanne and Carla weren't really keeping track of me. Besides, the most convincing detail is the cell phone location data that shows I never left Woodside."

"Or, rather, that your phone never left Woodside," says Winnie. "How many problems do you think you've solved by simply leaving your cell phone behind?" She can see Ava laugh with her whole body.

It was a smart move on her friend's part—planting her cell phone in the medicine cabinet of the guest bathroom while she took a Lyft to South San Francisco, did the deal, and then came right back. Her alibi was impenetrable; the detective lapped it all up.

Another point in their favor: Boss Mak has confessed

to the charges. To clear his daughter's name, he's owned up to running a black factory in his own legitimate factory's backyard, brazenly copying the blueprints entrusted to him by the world's most exclusive brands. As promised, the detective has garnered Ava a good plea bargain from the prosecutor.

And yet, and yet, in this business there are no guarantees. The threat of an overzealous judge holding some unknown bias or grudge looms over them all.

Soon Ava starts to yawn, and Winnie says, "You should get some rest," to which her friend replies, "If we win, the adrenaline will keep me going for another week. If we lose, I'll have plenty of time to sleep in jail."

Winnie's skull seems to contract as though caught in a vise. "Don't even joke about that."

"Relax," Ava says. "It's all we have right now."

THROUGHOUT THE MORNING WINNIE PACES the length of her living room, too antsy to consume anything, not even her customary double espresso. Every few minutes she checks the time. Ava should be in court, maybe rising to her feet at this very moment to receive her sentence.

In search of distractions, Winnie turns on the television, landing on a game show involving an eligible young bachelor, charged to choose a date from a group of attractive women (hidden behind a curtain) by interviewing only their mothers. The moms are touchingly cutthroat as they disparage the other daughters to spotlight their own, but the host's braying voice grates on Winnie, and she turns the TV off.

She paces the living room until her legs grow sore. What is taking Ava so long to call? The hearing is supposed to be straightforward, in and out.

Her phone emits a piercing ring. She flies at it. "Well?"

Ava's voice pours into her ear. She talks so fast and so loud that Winnie has to tell her to slow down and enunciate.

"Back up," Winnie says. "I want all the details."

Ava starts over. Picture her in a new dress purchased for the occasion: somber, black, elbow-length sleeves, a skirt that ends midcalf. She even changed her hair for the first time in twenty years.

"It's so short it barely grazes my earlobes. No greater symbol of remorse than a woman shorn, right?"

When Judge Lincoln Kramer began his sentencing statement, Ava was so nervous she thought she might faint right there on the courtroom floor. It didn't help that the judge possessed a particularly booming, gravelly voice, as though the Judeo-Christian God himself were sitting up there on the bench, ready to mete out judgment.

Ava's hopes fell when the judge described how she and the despicable Winnie Fang—his exact words—had duped scores of innocent people out of hundreds of thousands of dollars. Her hopes rose when the judge cited her willingness to give up the counterfeits kingpin, Mak Yiu Fai. They rose higher still when he pointed to her pristine background—her lack of a prior record, her stellar education and employment history, her stable family situation. And when he concluded that it was clear from the way she readily and voluntarily acknowledged her guilt that she had no apparent predisposition to behave criminally, but had been induced by Winnie Fang to participate in this particular crime under circumstances of coercion, her hopes soared to stratospheric heights.

"At this time, Ms. Wong," he boomed, "after looking at the evidence and weighing the allegations, I believe I can see who you really are."

Ava kept her eyes downcast, her expression solemn, her entire posture contrite.

"As such, I am giving you two years' probation, plus restitutions of five hundred thousand dollars."

At this, she lost control and lifted her gaze to meet the judge's. Tears cascaded down her cheeks like so many loose gemstones. It was the absolute lightest sentence they could have wished for.

"I'm confident you won't make the same mistakes again and commit another crime. Don't prove me wrong, young lady."

Through her tears, she said, "I won't, sir, you have my word, sir."

"Winnie?" Ava yells into the phone now. "Did I lose you?"

"I'm right here," Winnie says. What else is there to add? Ava's proven to be a straight-A student through and through.

To celebrate, Winnie allows herself a nonessential errand,

walking a little farther to the high-end wineshop to buy a nice bottle of champagne. On her way back, she spots a familiar hulking figure, talking to the apartment complex's security guard. She ducks into a bus stop and pretends to study the schedule. The big man is wearing a baseball cap. She can't say for certain it's the same guy. She waits in the bus stop until the man ambles off and then she approaches the guardhouse.

"Good afternoon, Miss Zhou," the guard says. "Have you eaten yet?"

"Yes, and you?" she replies. "By the way, who was that man you were talking to earlier? He looks familiar, like someone I knew in my hometown."

"Where are you from?" he asks.

"Xiamen." She shifts the bag with the champagne from one hand to the other.

"Ah, I don't think it's him, then. His accent sounded Cantonese."

The skin on her forearms prickles. "I see. And what did he want?"

"He runs a landscaping business and wanted to know if we were looking for gardeners. I told him to contact the owners. What do I know? I'm just the guard."

"True," she says, "true."

IN THE FOLLOWING WEEKS, THE Chinese press maintains that Boss Mak's confession was coerced. This, Winnie knows, is a good sign; he has the government's support. She anticipates that Mak International will be slapped with a sizable fine and subjected to a few years of heightened inspections to appease the international brands, nothing too serious. Sure, they'll lose clients in the short term, but, with time, the brands will be back, unable to resist the cost savings.

Resolving to listen to Ava, Winnie stays off social media and focuses on their new venture. After several more fruitless meetings, including one in which a greasy sales manager implies that if he and Winnie were to become *good friends*, he'd make an exception and work with her, she finally signs a contract with a small but growing diamond manufacturer that she hopes could be their partner for years to come. Her decision was made the moment the head of sales, a woman around Winnie's age, pressed a business card with her personal cell number into Winnie's palm, saying, "Don't hesitate to call or text if you need anything at all," and she knew for certain that there was nothing untoward about it.

With that settled, she prepares to return to America.

Winnie wouldn't have based her fictional jewelry business in Hopkinton, New Hampshire, if she hadn't thought she'd like to live there. She makes an offer on a house, a classic Cape Cod–style brick cottage. It's simple and symmetrical—basically what Henri would produce if told to draw a house—and a world away from the steel and glass of her old L.A. condo. The cottage stands on the quaint-sounding Spruce Lane. She imagines unhurried evening walks down her street, waving at neighbors, who'll probably take her for one of those FIRE millennials — Financial Independence, Retire Early. Why not encourage that misconception? She can tell them she made a bunch of money in tech and then moved here to reconnect with the land: to grow her own vegetables, learn to butcher, write a blog on zero waste.

So what if she's never been to New Hampshire and can see neither the town nor the house in person? The brisk, perky real estate agent has assured her that both are move-in ready, and not to worry about the flagpole by the door, she can have that taken down before Winnie arrives.

In truth, though Winnie would never admit it to the agent, she loves the American flag planted out front, along with the Shaker-style cabinetry and wood-plank walls. She's even asked to keep the previous owners' floor-length chintz drapes. The agent has said that the sellers are a pair of retired schoolteachers who taught for years at a ritzy boarding school in the neighboring town. Winnie imagines them to be white haired and ruddy cheeked, hale and outdoorsy in plaid work shirts and khakis. The couple has cultivated a lovely rustic garden, with lush azalea and dogwood trees, which Winnie will learn to maintain. In all her life, she's never had a garden of her own, and three hundred and sixty thousand dollars in cash seems a more than fair price to pay for that privilege.

Through this time, she continues to leave the apartment

complex only when necessary, always looking out for the beat-up Nissan and the hulking man, but she doesn't see them again.

One morning, a headline on the *New York Times* website grabs her attention: LVMH TO PULL OUT OF CHINA. From the subsequent article she learns that recent revelations at Mak International have prompted LVMH to threaten to cease doing business with Chinese factories, and the other luxury conglomerates indicate they'll follow suit.

All at once, the narrative in the Chinese media shifts. When Winnie turns on CCTV, she finds an exposé on Mandy Mak's lavish lifestyle. The first-class trips to Paris and Milan, the collection of Manolo Blahniks, the new lipstick-red Tesla—it's all right there for everyone to gawk at. The one photo that the news channels keep trotting out has been lifted straight from her Instagram account: Mandy in an orange bikini, lounging on the deck of a gleaming yacht, surrounded by the iconic white cliffside houses of Santorini.

The outrage on Weibo is instantaneous.

The Maks and the rest of those corrupt tycoons are a stain on our nation.

The international brands will never trust us again, all because of those greedy bloodsuckers.

The rich think they can get away with everything. Lock them up!

From *Liberation Daily* Winnie learns that the vice mayor of Guangzhou has been demoted to director of sanitation, that the former police chief is under investigation for graft.

For the first time in weeks, she checks Mandy's social media accounts. The last post is a photo snapped at the previous month's press conference captioned, *Thank you all for the support. I won't rest until my dad is free.* Mandy Mak has gone dark.

Has she left social media to focus on saving her father, or has she been detained at a resort hotel in some remote locale with no access to the outside world? Either way, all signs point to a colossal public reckoning, to the kind of scapegoating that will destroy the Maks and their associates forever — Winnie included, if her whereabouts are discovered by the government or the Maks' henchmen, or both.

She sends a text message to her graphic design contact, telling him there's been a change of plans, she needs that passport ASAP. She ties her scarf around her head, puts on her coat and sunglasses, and leaves the apartment. Outside, at the end of the block, she bursts through the door of a small hair salon she's passed many times before. It's a dingy, spartan place, the sole employee a middle-aged woman with a halo of permed curls, lounging in one of the vinyl chairs.

"Miss, are you sure?" she asks after hearing Winnie's instructions.

"Very," Winnie says. "I've been planning this for months."

"All right then," the stylist says doubtfully, fingering a thick lock of Winnie's nipple-length mane. "It's just hair, right? It'll grow back."

Winnie leaves the salon half an hour later, newly unrecognizable with her fresh cut. Despite the woman's own questionable sense of style, she's given Winnie exactly what she asked for—a tousled pixie with wispy baby bangs.

At the end of the week, Winnie boards a 787 Dreamliner bound for Newark. Walking down the aisle, she scans the business-class cabin, half expecting to see the hulking man. Once she's stowed away her hand luggage and taken her seat, she declines the flight attendant's offer of a pre-takeoff beverage, keeping her eyes trained on the passenger door.

"Don't be nervous. Flying is safer than driving," the man seated across the aisle says.

He's an American, probably in Beijing on business, probably something tech related, judging from his flawless white Nikes and expensive sweats.

"Who said I was afraid of flying?" Winnie says.

He's the loud, friendly type who loves the sound of his own voice. He lets out a guffaw, but falls silent when she doesn't even crack a smile. She turns to the window to discourage him from continuing the conversation and is heartened when he starts in with the passenger on his other side.

Every time the flight attendants confer with one another, or with a pilot, or with a gate agent, Winnie shrinks into her seat, even as Ava's voice replays in her head. *Nobody but me has any idea where you are. Nobody but me. Nobody. Nobody. Nobody. Me.*

"Will you be joining us for dinner this evening?" the flight attendant asks.

Although Winnie can't imagine ingesting a single bite right now, she nods her head yes.

"And did you have a chance to peruse the menu?"

Winnie shakes her head no. Her tongue is a slab of raw meat; it seems to fill her entire mouth. Making an effort to enunciate, she says, "Whatever the vegetarian option is — I'll have that."

Eventually, the passengers fasten their seat belts, and the doors close, and the cabin crew takes their seats. An eternity later, the plane ambles down the runway, gaining speed before, at last, lifting into the sky.

Winnie exhales. It's mid-December and the city below is gray and bleak. Within the month the residents of Beijing will wake to a rare blanketing of snow, and children will swarm these streets to play. Within the month Mandy Mak will be photographed returning to her Dongguan town house, and Kaiser Shih, the alleged mastermind behind it all, will be taken into police custody.

At this moment, however, Winnie thinks only of her new garden, napping beneath the frost, awaiting the first murmurs of spring. Before turning off her phone, she types a short message to Ava: I'm coming home.

EPILOGUE

The day she's free to leave the jurisdiction, Ava kisses her son goodbye. She feels jittery, unsettled, as though she's forgotten something important, even though she's gone over her packing list again and again. She hasn't been more than an hour's drive from Henri in the entire time she's been on probation, though her son clearly shares none of her anxiety, seeing as he's already gone back to his Magna-Tiles.

Two years earlier, following her sentencing hearing, Ava began divorce proceedings and moved with Henri to an apartment in Lower Pac Heights. At first she feared her son would balk at the lack of space. To this day, however, he can while away hours sitting by the window overlooking Bush Street, watching the cars rush past. Her own time is spent as a receptionist at a dental clinic in the neighborhood—employment being a requirement of her probation. She doesn't mind the work, answering phone calls, checking in the patients who come to see the brusque, no-nonsense dentist. The other day the dentist gave her a whole bag of sugar-free lollipops to take home to Henri. He's the only one who offered her a job despite her criminal record.

She crouches down beside her son. "Are you building a cave?" she asks. "A racetrack? A roller coaster?"

He goes on snapping one plastic tile to another.

She checks her phone and sees that her Lyft is still several minutes away. "Please answer me when I talk to you."

"It's a bus depot, Mama."

Her heart seizes. She looks at Maria with pride. Every day Henri comes up with new words, she has no idea how. After a year and a half of weekly appointments, his speech therapist has suggested they drop down to monthly, just to check in. She kisses the top of his head one last time and gets up.

"Oli's number is on the fridge," she tells Maria.

"I know."

"I'll call every night at six."

"Okay."

"Oli will pick him up on Friday night and bring him back Sunday night."

"Ava," Maria says. "We've been over this."

"Right, right."

She will always be grateful to Maria for coming back. Initially, even the offer of full-time pay for part-time work—Henri's in school until one in the afternoon—had failed to move her. At last Ava trotted out the speech she'd given to family, friends, prospective employers: That

Winnie had preyed on her vulnerability, manipulated her into committing a crime. That this turbulent period was firmly behind her. She might even have sandwiched Maria's hand in both of hers and said, "You of all people know the real me."

And how had Maria responded? For a beat she cocked her head and studied Ava, and then an enormous rollicking laugh filled the room, bouncing off the walls, reverberating in Ava's ears.

What? Ava wanted to ask. What's so funny?

Maria laughed and laughed, clutching her stomach, gasping for breath, wiping actual tears from the corners of her eyes like a goddamn emoji. "Ava," she said, "that good-immigrant shit may work on white people, but it won't work on me."

Regaining composure, she issued her one condition: that Ava refrain from talking about her work, her day, her mood. If it didn't have to do with Henri, Maria didn't want to know about it.

Ava put aside her hurt feelings and agreed.

Now she kisses Henri one last time.

"Bye-bye, Mama," he says in his raspy Rod Stewart voice.

She slips on her shoes and takes the handle of her Rollaboard.

"If you see Auntie Winnie, can you tell her I miss her?"

Ava whips around to face her son. The mangled mink ball from all those years ago dangles from his fingers.

Where did he find it? Did she even pack it when they moved? "Auntie Winnie doesn't live here anymore, remember? Mama doesn't see her."

"I know, Mama," he says, stuffing the ball in the pocket of his shorts. "I just meant *if*."

Ava glances at Maria, stricken. She's bustling around the living room, picking up stray toys. "Get out of here," she calls. "I didn't hear a thing."

THE MANCHESTER AIRPORT IS BARE-BONES: a single terminal, worn carpeting, minimal security. Ava combs the arrival hall, wondering if she'll recognize her friend's altered face. And then there she is! Bundled into one of those sleeping-bag down coats, her pixie cut tucked beneath a fuzzy beanie, Winnie's once again her college roommate, all buzzing energy and insatiable curiosity.

When their eyes lock, Ava feels her cheeks warm. She's inexplicably shy. Her hand flies up to her own strands, snipped to just below the earlobe, which Winnie has not yet seen. She liked the haircut so much, she's kept it ever since her sentencing hearing.

"Nice hair," says Winnie.

"Nice face," Ava replies.

And then—she's not sure which of them initiates it— their arms wrap around each other, and she takes a deep whiff of her friend, who smells not like expensive eau de toilette, but like grass, rain, woodsmoke. She's a shapeshifter, this Winnie, a wholehearted embracer of whatever

her circumstances. She's so fully herself that the changes
only seem to further solidify who she really is.

Ava says, "I can't believe we're really here."

"I can," says Winnie.

"Oh, please. I'm the one who said this would work."

"But I'm the one who knew you had it in you." Winnie
threads her arm through Ava's, and they touch their heads
and laugh.

En route to the parking lot, Winnie tells Ava about her
new home. Her neighbors are delightful, so warm and wel-
coming. She's thinking of getting a golden retriever. She
can't wait to show Ava the charming ancient shops on Main
Street. Through it all, Ava listens for a hint of sarcasm,
mockery, and finds none.

At Winnie's house, Ava spies the American flag by the
front door and giggles.

"What?" Winnie says. "It came with the place, and
frankly I quite like it."

They settle in the living room on the blue-and-white-
striped overstuffed sofa.

Ava says, "I thought I saw him again, the other day,
walking down the block." She tells Winnie she jumped behind a pillar, quaking, before getting a hold of herself.

Winnie reminds Ava that Kaiser Shih won't be eligible
for parole for another four years, and the rest of them—
Mandy, the police chief, the vice mayor—would never
risk coming to the US. Still reeling from the government
crackdown, they fear for their own freedom more than

they begrudge Ava hers. It's nothing Winnie hasn't said before.

"I know, I know," says Ava. "But my subconscious has ideas of its own."

"Tell your subconscious that I'm the one they really want, if only they could figure out where I am."

Ava's gaze sweeps the room, all pastel florals and dark wood. "Well, this certainly is the last place they'd imagine finding you."

Winnie smirks. "He wouldn't have been surprised." Her eyes mist over. She means Boss Mak, of course. He's been gone for almost two years, his liver finally failing him a month after his arrest.

Ava hurries to comfort her. "Oli says the medical team did everything possible to relieve his pain at the end. He didn't suffer." It's nothing she hasn't said before either.

"So did you meet the new fiancée?" Winnie asks.

Ava waggles her head from side to side. "She came with Oli to pick up Henri a couple weeks ago but didn't get out of the car. I think she's good for him. He seems calmer, less angry. And Henri likes her too." Mimi, her son calls her, short for Myriam. It unsettled Ava the first time she heard the nickname, not because she was jealous, but because it gave her a glimpse into her son's inner life, a burgeoning side to him of which she has no part.

"Of course Oli's less angry. Isn't she a resident? She probably lets him order her around."

"Stop," says Ava, but she appreciates her friend's loyalty all the same.

Winnie brings out a bottle of pinot noir that she pours into two large goblets. Together they sit and sip, watching the shadows lengthen across the parquet floor.

"I almost forgot," Winnie says. She goes to the hall closet and returns with something in a plain white dust bag, which she sets in Ava's lap.

"What's this?" Ava's nostrils flare at some faint animal scent. Her pulse quickens. Her fingers race to loosen the drawstring opening and pull out the blood-red crocodile Birkin.

The last time she saw this bag, it was being tossed in the back of a moving van, along with the other valuables confiscated by the Department of Homeland Security.

Ava asks, "How did you get this?"

"I waited for them to auction it off."

Ava turns the bag this way and that. The crocodile skin retains its pristine mirrorlike gloss. The plastic protective tape on the palladium hardware is still intact. "How much did you pay?"

"Who cares?" Winnie swats her with an accent pillow. "It has sentimental value."

Ava's never heard her friend speak so cavalierly about money, and when she points this out, Winnie shrugs. "That's because I don't get attached to any old object. Without the emotions and the stories, they're just *things*."

Ava knows exactly what she means. The bag's never

been used and likely never will be, but she will keep it forever as a talisman, a symbol of her fearlessness and verve,
of everything Winnie has taught her.

"I have something for you, too," Ava says. She unzips
her suitcase and retrieves a plain padded mailer, hands it to
Winnie.

Inside, wrapped in tissue, is a lab-grown three-carat
round loose diamond the size of a fingernail. It sparkles like
a meteor in Winnie's palm. Ava snaps on a light, while Winnie pulls out her jewelry loupe and tweezers and examines
the stone. As promised, it is perfect—perfectly irregular,
perfectly flawed, ready to be swapped in for a natural diamond set in an elegant platinum band.

This time around, they will hire men, all of marrying
age; men who'll report solely to them. And when their handsome, strapping shopper walks into Tiffany's or Chopard
or Harry Winston to return the engagement ring—utterly
dejected over his would-be fiancée's no—what sales associate wouldn't want to be useful, to soothe his hurt feelings,
and help make things right?

"Exquisite," Winnie says, lowering the stone to the table. "We'll start in Boston next month."

In the lamplight, the diamond winks like a girl with a
secret.

"Okay," Ava says, "once and for all, tell me how you did
it. How did you buy your SAT score?"

Winnie nearly spits out her wine like an actor in a sit-
com. She throws back her head and cackles—there's no

other word for the pure shrill sound that tumbles out of her, making Ava wonder if this small-town solitude has turned her strange.

At last, Winnie sets down her glass. "I didn't pay anyone. That test is a joke."

Instantly Ava regrets bringing it up. She chokes out, "I'm so sorry, I didn't know . . . your dad . . . he really had a stroke?"

"No, Dad was fine," Winnie says. "Those princelings paid *me* to take their tests. That's how I got a perfect score. Practice. That's how I could afford to go to Stanford."

"You're kidding."

"That stuff pays well. Didn't you read the news reports?"

"What about your scholarship? And your aunt?"

Winnie rolls her eyes extravagantly. "That barely covered tuition. There was still room and board, textbooks, health insurance."

And then it's Ava who's cackling, toasting her friend, and then toasting this mad and maddening country of theirs.

At first, she'd tried to discourage Winnie from coming back. It seemed safer, less complicated for her to remain outside the US in Geneva, say, or Buenos Aires, or Mexico City. There was no reason for them to be in the same place. But when Winnie called to say she'd found this house, Ava knew it could be no other way. Winnie loved Boss Mak—Ava has never doubted that—but she loved America more. This was where she belonged, with the weirdest of the weird and the boldest of the bold. Winnie's the one who showed Ava her country for what it truly is: a wild-fire, a head-on collision, a spooked horse that's thrown off its rider, a motherfucking driverless car. It's the only place for freaks like them, hucksters, con men, unicorns, queens. Winnie is the American dream, and that's what drives everyone mad, mad, mad—that she had the gall to crash their game and win it all.

Now it's Winnie's turn to wonder what Ava finds so funny.

The laughter empties out of her, but Ava is filled to the brim. "That we did it," she says. "That we won the whole damn thing."

They clink glasses, drain their wine, and get down to business.

ACKNOWLEDGMENTS

Thank you to Michelle Brower, Jessica Williams, Danya Kukafka, Ore Agbaje-Williams, Julia Elliott, Allison Warren, and everyone at Aevitas Creative Management, William Morrow, and The Borough Press. To Kim Liao, Beth Nguyen, Reese Kwon, and Aimee Phan. To the National Arts Council of Singapore, the Creative Writing Programme at Nanyang Technological University, and the Toji Cultural Center. To the many books that helped me complete this novel, especially *Deluxe: How Luxury Lost Its Luster* by Dana Thomas, *Factory Girls: From Village to City in a Changing China* by Leslie T. Chang, and *Blood Profits: How American Consumers Unwittingly Fund Terrorists* by Vanessa Neumann. To Kathy Shih, Stephen Lin, and the late Yvonne Chua. To Nelson Luo, Eric Zhou, Shirley Nie, and everyone at Sitoy Group. To trusted early reader and all-around sounding board Vanessa Hua. To Matthew Salesses, my guiding light. To my parents and my family. And, always, to Asmin.

6-22

14733

MS